PENGUIN CLASSICS

THE VINLAND SAGAS

Born and raised in Winnipeg, Canada, KENEVA KUNZ studied Germanic languages and linguistics in Manitoba, Munich and Copenhagen, where her doctoral thesis examined translation of Icelandic medieval sagas. In addition to teaching translation for several years at the University of Iceland, she has worked as translator and editor in Reykjavík, Brussels and Stockholm since 1987.

GÍSLI SIGURÐSSON (b. 1959) is from Reykjavík, Iceland. He is a research professor at the Árni Magnússon Institute in Iceland with a long-standing interest in oral tradition and orally derived texts, particularly in the areas of medieval literature and folk tales and folklore of more recent times. His publications include many articles for academic journals both within and outside Iceland, the study *Gaelic Influence in Iceland: Historical and Literary Contacts, A Survey of Research* (1988, reissued 2000), a full annotated edition of the ancient Edda poems, *Eddukvæði* (1998), and *The Medieval Icelandic Saga and Oral Tradition: A Discourse on Method* (2004). Gísli has a wife and two daughters and lives in Reykjavík.

WORLD OF THE SAGAS

Editor Örnólfur Thorsson
Assistant Editor † Bernard Scudder

The Vinland Sagas

The Icelandic Sagas about the First Documented Voyages across the North Atlantic

The Saga of the Greenlanders
and
Eirik the Red's Saga

Translated by KENEVA KUNZ
With an Introduction and Notes by
GÍSLI SIGURÐSSON

PENGUIN BOOKS

PENGUIN CLASSICS

Published by the Penguin Group
Penguin Books Ltd, 80 Strand, London WC2R ORL, England
Penguin Group (USA) Inc., 375 Hudson Street, New York, New York 10014, USA
Penguin Group (Canada), 90 Eglinton Avenue East, Suite 700, Toronto, Ontario, Canada M4P 2Y3
(a division of Pearson Penguin Canada Inc.)
Penguin Ireland, 25 St Stephen's Green, Dublin 2, Ireland (a division of Penguin Books Ltd)
Penguin Group (Australia), 250 Camberwell Road, Camberwell, Victoria 3124, Australia
(a division of Pearson Australia Group Pty Ltd)
Penguin Books India Pvt Ltd, 11 Community Centre, Panchsheel Park, New Delhi – 110 017, India
Penguin Group (NZ), 67 Apollo Drive, Rosedale, North Shore 0632, New Zealand
(a division of Pearson New Zealand Ltd)
Penguin Books (South Africa) (Pty) Ltd, 24 Sturdee Avenue, Rosebank, Johannesburg 2196, South Africa

Penguin Books Ltd, Registered Offices: 80 Strand, London WC2R ORL, England

www.penguin.com

Translations first published in *The Complete Sagas of Icelanders (Including 49 Tales)*, I,
edited by Viðar Hreinsson (General Editor), Robert Cook, Terry Gunnell, Keneva Kunz
and Bernard Scudder. Leifur Eiríksson Publishing Ltd, Iceland 1997
First published in Penguin Classics 2008

029

Translation copyright © Leifur Eiríksson, 1997
Editorial material copyright © Gísli Sigurðsson, 2008
All rights reserved

The moral right of the translator and editor has been asserted

Leifur Eiríksson Publishing Ltd gratefully acknowledges the support of the
Nordic Cultural Fund, Ariane Programme of the European Union, UNESCO,
Icelandair and others.

The map on p. 000 and the table on p. 000 were first published in Gísli Sigurðsson's *The
Medieval Icelandic Saga and Oral Tradition* (2004); Gísli Sigurðsson and the publishers
gratefully acknowledge the permission of the Publications of the Milman Parry Collection of
Oral Literature to reproduce them in this volume.

Set in 10.25/12.25 pt PostScript Adobe Sabon
Typeset by Rowland Phototypesetting Ltd, Bury St Edmunds, Suffolk
Printed and bound in Great Britain by Clays Ltd, Elcograf S.p.A.

ISBN: 978-0-140-44776-7

www.greenpenguin.co.uk

MIX
Paper from
responsible sources
FSC
www.fsc.org   FSC® C018179

Penguin Books is committed to a sustainable
future for our business, our readers and our planet.
This book is made from Forest Stewardship
Council™ certified paper.

Contents

Acknowledgements

My study of the Vinland Sagas took off in earnest in Spring 1996 when I spent time as a Nordplus lecturer at the University of Nuuk in Greenland. Its university library contained a good selection of books on Norse finds in Greenland and at L'Anse aux Meadows in Newfoundland, which I could delve into, and I had the great benefit of being able to discuss these matters with the rector of the university, Claus Andreasen, who was himself an archaeologist. Another source of inspiration was Harry Baglole, director of the Institute of Island Studies at the University of Prince Edward Island. He showed great interest in my developing ideas when we first met in Reykjavík shortly after my stay in Greenland, and arranged for lecture tours and field trips in and around his island. The millennium celebrations called for a special focus on Vinland studies with exhibitions and publications commemorating the voyage of Leif Eiriksson. I was involved with the preparations for the exhibition *Vikings: The North Atlantic Saga*, which visited several cities in North America under the supervision of the Smithsonian Institution, and was the curator for the exhibition *Vikings and the New World* in the Culture House in Reykjavík, with scenographer Sigurjón Jóhannsson. In this work I benefited greatly from the advice of William Fitzhugh and Elisabeth Ward, my editors at the Smithsonian Institution, and from my discussions with archaeologist Birgitta Wallace, who was exceptionally generous with her time when we first met on Prince Edward Island in Spring 1998 and has since written a number of long letters to me that have opened my eyes to many of the problems associated with Vinland studies. In addition I have had deep and lively

talks on the Vinland voyages with Páll Bergþórsson, which have
made me much clearer about the questions that need to be
addressed. As this work on Vinland proceeded I was well into
the writing of my book on orality and the Icelandic sagas
which was published in 2004, translated by Nicholas Jones, as
volume 2 in the Publications of the Milman Parry Collection
of Oral Literature at Harvard University under the title *The
Medieval Icelandic Saga and Oral Tradition: A Discourse on
Method*. As it turned out I was able to apply my thinking about
orality in the Middle Ages to many of the traditional problems
attached to the Vinland sagas – and to come up with some new
methods, approaches and even answers that I have made use
of in this volume. Finally my thanks go to Leifur Eiríksson
Publishing in Reykjavík, Jóhann Sigurðsson and Bernard
Scudder in particular, who have been instrumental in bringing
this volume out, Lindeth Vasey in particular, and the very
friendly and encouraging editorial staff at Penguin, in whose
hands much of what is said here has been polished and
sharpened.

Gísli Sigurðsson

In memory of
Bernard Scudder
29 August 1954–15 October 2007

Introduction

The *Vinland Sagas* are two separate works that were written down independently in Iceland in the early thirteenth century and belong to a literary genre known as *The Sagas of Icelanders*, none of which has an author's name associated with it. The *Vinland Sagas* contain the oldest descriptions of the North American continent and tell the story of several voyages undertaken by people from Iceland and Greenland to North America around the year 1000 – the first documented voyages across the Atlantic, in which the peoples of Europe and America met for the first time. The pioneering voyage, after a chance discovery of lands south and west of Greenland by the Icelandic merchant Bjarni Herjolfsson, was conducted by Leif Eiriksson to a land he named Vinland ('Wineland'). He was nicknamed 'the Lucky' after rescuing shipwrecked seamen on his way back (rescuing others is still considered a sign of luck among Icelandic seafarers), and later voyages were then led by Leif's brother Thorvald; by Thorfinn Karlsefni and Gudrid Thorbjarnardottir, the first European couple to have a child, Snorri, born in North America; and finally by Leif's half-sister Freydis Eiriksdottir, whose voyage ended in disaster.

Eirik the Red's Saga is preserved in two vellum manuscripts, *Hauksbók* (early fourteenth century) and *Skálholtsbók* (early fifteenth century). They were based on an original written after 1263[1] – which in turn was based on an older text from the early thirteenth century. The saga, in spite of its title, hardly tells anything about Eirik, but exalts the memory of Thorfinn Karlsefni (descended from Aud (Unn) the Deep-minded, a Viking queen in Dublin and settler in west Iceland at the opening of *The*

Saga of the People of Laxardal,[2] and Kjarval, King of Ireland); and Gudrid Thorbjarnardottir (descended from a Gaelic slave brought to Iceland by the same Aud), who finally settled in Iceland, where she, as an elderly woman, became a nun after a subsequent pilgrimage to Rome.

The Saga of the Greenlanders is preserved as a part of a larger work about King Olaf Tryggvason in the vellum manuscript *Flateyjarbók*, from around 1387,[3] from an original written much earlier, very likely at the beginning of the thirteenth century. It lacks a beginning introducing Eirik the Red's settlement in Iceland and Greenland, which had been included by the scribe in the previous chapter of Olaf's saga, using the so-called *Sturlubók* version of *The Book of Settlements*, but the opening is not included here as the information can be found in Chapter 2 of *Eirik the Red's Saga*. *The Saga of the Greenlanders* focuses on Leif the Lucky's leading role in the Vinland voyages and includes a striking and memorable account of the vicious Freydis.

INSPIRATION AND LITERARY COMPOSITION

Both the *Vinland Sagas* reflect genuine family traditions and mention that three bishops in the twelfth and thirteenth centuries could trace their families back to Gudrid and Thorfinn Karlsefni through Snorri, the first 'Vinlander', and his brother (Thor) Bjorn. The emphasis on the bishops among the descendants is thematically part of the conflict between the old pagan culture and Christianity which is so prominent in the Vinland sagas, Eirik's saga in particular, where Leif Eiriksson is commissioned by King Olaf Tryggvason to convert the heathen settlers of Greenland to Christianity. Often the conflicting beliefs struggle for ascendancy: for instance, the Christian Gudrid, who agrees to take part in sorcery to help people in need, and the prayers of the voyagers to North America for God's help after rejecting succour from Thor. The names of Gudrid and

Freydis also point to the conflict: *Gud-* alludes to the Christian God, while Frey and Freyja were heathen fertility gods. Freydis's outrageous behaviour is thus linked to heathendom, the antithesis of Gudrid's Christian kindness.

The story of Gudrid and Thorfinn Karlsefni's love knits *Eirik the Red's Saga* together. They come from different backgrounds: he is of noble birth and his name derives from the thunder-god Thor, while she is of humble origins but devout in her faith. Their relationship begins under strange circumstances in Greenland, and then they return to the established order of society in Iceland and move in with his family. It is only natural that Thorfinn's mother should give a lukewarm reception to her low-born daughter-in-law – but Gudrid will compensate through her faith, to become a worthy foremother of bishops. Generally speaking, the purpose of written sagas is linked with the interests of the patrons of the writers. The emphasis on Gudrid's devout Christianity, which she takes to the end of the known world and back, is connected with the naming of the bishops in the closing chapters, who presumably saw benefits in championing the memory of the voyages to Vinland and their remote association with them. With a foremother of such character they could consolidate their position in society and gain further respect and honour.

It also seems likely that the main natural resources remembered from Vinland, wild grapes and self-sown wheat, are linked to Christian practices: since the holy sacrament requires wine and flour (for the bread), it was quite valuable to be able to prove that the distant settlements in Greenland had access to them. Nor is it surprising that the accounts of Vinland contain many echoes of early Irish ideas about a land of plenty to the west and medieval writings about Paradise. The world of the Icelandic sagas, from Greenland, Iceland, Scandinavia, the British Isles and mainland Europe all the way south and east to Russia and Constantinople, was known to the writers of the sagas through the journeys of their contemporaries as well as from books. The impulse to tell stories about this world and set themselves in it may thus be related to the fact that this was a known world and a known setting. Though there was no written information about North America, let alone first-hand contemporary accounts of journeys – though this idea has been mooted[4] – people wrote sagas about voyages to these places in which the geography and inhabitants are described in some detail. So where did the saga writers get their information?

Many of the people who emigrated to Greenland and were active in the Vinland voyages were descended from settlers in the Breidafjord area (west Iceland) – and many of those, in turn, were of British/Gaelic descent. Some would undoubtedly have been familiar with Irish tales of legendary, magical lands in the western ocean, lands of plenty where the tellers envisaged beautiful women, inexhaustible wine, rivers full of enormous salmon and everlasting bliss. These highly fanciful tales have features reminiscent of the mythical *Ódáinsvellir* ('Fields of the Undying') described in Norse sources, where those who managed to get to these wonderful lands had no way back to this earthly life. Tales preserved in *The Book of Settlements* and later sources of a voyage by Ari Masson and other men from Breidafjord to a place called 'Land of the White Men' may perhaps owe something to such legends, and it is possible that such stories may have encouraged people to sail west in search of lands beyond the sea.[5] For instance, *The Book of Settlements* records that in the first party that moved to Greenland with Eirik the Red was a Christian man from the Hebrides, while according to *Eirik the Red's Saga*, Karlsefni's crew included Leif's slaves from Scotland, a man and woman named Haki and Hekja. Since the North American flora and climate bore distinct similarities to the descriptions in these legends, it is well conceivable that fact and fiction became merged in the telling and led people to believe they had found these wonderful lands. However, the Irish legends cannot explain the many realistic features of the *Vinland Sagas*. However much these sagas may owe in their form to the travel sagas such as *The Saga of Yngvar the Widely-Travelled*,[6] which takes its characters deep into Russia, to the Black Sea and even as far as the Caspian region, there is a vast difference between the descriptions of the lands to the west of the Atlantic and the stories of the East where men capture cities and fight against kings. Such exotica in relation to faraway lands are entirely absent from the *Vinland Sagas* and, in the absence of exaggeration, it is tempting to see reality and hard fact – and say that, if such wonders do not appear in the *Vinland Sagas*, it is because they did not appear in Vinland.

SAGAS AND SOCIAL MEMORY

Great events first become noteworthy when someone tells their story. *The Sagas of Icelanders* offer the reader extraordinarily accessible prose narratives from an ancient culture; very old in subject matter but very modern in approach. Written in Iceland in the thirteenth and fourteenth centuries by unknown individuals who give every saga its personal flavour in content and in style, and prefiguring the European novel, they also present us with a window to the times when the stories that make up a saga were told and retold by traditional storytellers, reshaped and changed according to the needs of the audience and the abilities of the teller. They give us a glimpse back to when some of the events described actually took place – and thus triggered the first story. As a result we have saga texts that contain a mixture of fact and fiction, the merging of the oral and the written, where the traditional and the individual meet. They were written by Christians about their pagan ancestors, using the literary technique brought to them by the Church, in order to present their own heritage, drawing on the only available sources: their elders. The writers' relation to the oral tradition might explain why we know so little about them: most likely they did not regard themselves as authors in the modern sense. Rather they were assembling and writing down from tradition what was common knowledge at the time – even though we can now detect many literary features and authorial intent in their compositions.

The Sagas of Icelanders, one literary genre of many in medieval Iceland, comprise forty prose narratives that fill five volumes in the Leifur Eiríksson English translation,[7] and tell of the Icelanders themselves during the first centuries of settlement in their country. They often start in Norway and follow the main characters across the sea to Iceland, where they face the difficulties and hardships of life in a new land. In these sagas the new religion Christianity brings a peaceful solution to long-lasting blood feuds that had led to one revenge killing after the other, and to internal family struggles in which the laws of duty bring family members in deadly opposition to each other – although the pagan forefathers are in no way condemned for their religion, since they did not know any better from the point of view of the Christian saga writer.

What is so fascinating about the sagas is that many are exceptionally well-composed pieces of literature. They are often more accessible to the modern reader than the medieval literature most commonly known from other countries, such as the *chansons de geste* from France, or the courtly romances. What catches our attention is that their world is so coherent and often so realistic that many commentators have been tempted to regard them as descriptions of real life, even though they were all supposed to have taken place two or three hundred years before they were written. Saga genealogies match each other: the same chieftains appear, and the same laws and customs are given, in unrelated sagas – together giving the impression that the tales are describing a real society which we can reconstruct, using them as field reports. Characters are not only literary prototypes, as is often the case in heroic literature, but also flesh-and-blood people whom we seem to know as well as our old schoolmates. Today many are family friends in Icelandic homes, and are quoted for their wit and expressions of deep feelings of sorrow and joy.

Some sagas were written about Scandinavian kings and earls as well as about legendary heroes roaming around in the Viking Age (800–1050) (not to mention other kinds of literature, such as religious works, translations of well-known European texts and writings about contemporary events in Iceland). They describe a period when the peoples of mainland Scandinavia used their superior ships to win power and influence across the Baltic Sea to Russia, and as far south as the Caspian Sea and Constantinople. They also crossed the North Sea to the British

Isles, including Ireland, where they established colonies in Dublin, York and the Orkneys. Eventually they ventured farther into the North Atlantic and reached the Faroe Islands and, in 874, Iceland (both had also been visited sporadically by Irish hermits). About a hundred years later, the Icelanders continued on to Greenland and then to the North American continent, where they named the territories they found, from north to south: Helluland (Slab-stone land), Markland (Forest land) and Vinland. This ultimate destination was reached just over two hundred years after the first attack by Norwegian seafarers on the monastery of Lindisfarne off the east coast of England in 793 (generally seen as the start of the Viking Age). The Vikings were fearsome warriors who combined their lust for trade and warfare with the quest for new lands, which they explored, settled and ruled. Their scope for expansion seemed almost limitless until they were finally outnumbered by the natives in North America. After a few years of attempting settlement they took to the sea again, thus postponing further European influence in North America for five hundred years. The general outline for this history was preserved in the oral tradition and served as the background for the storytellers' creativity.

Even though the *Vinland Sagas* are literary works, they are based on oral memory and are not creative literature, nor are they historical documents. There is no doubt that the *Vinland Sagas* contain memories of real characters and events. But very likely they were not exactly as we are told in the sagas – which also disagree on some details and contain material which we would now classify as fanciful and supernatural. The sagas are still our best proof that such voyages to the North American continent took place. Coincidence or wishful thinking simply could not have produced descriptions of topography, natural resources and native lifestyles unknown to people in Europe that can be corroborated in North America. There is no need for archaeological evidence, rune stones or the Vinland Map to prove that basic fact.[8]

SOURCE VALUE AND METHODOLOGY

Our main source of information about the settlement of Iceland is Icelandic writings, supplemented by both archaeological evidence and writings of foreign historians. Strong doubts have sometimes been raised about the credibility of Icelandic writings from the twelfth and thirteenth centuries – *The Book of the Icelanders* (1122–32) by Ari the Learned and *The Book of Settlements* – given that they describe events supposed to have taken place two to four centuries earlier. Living oral traditions in many parts of the world show a tendency to adapt to contemporary reality, whereby facts are changed according to context even though people consider themselves to be preserving memories from the past; but despite this mutability, there is a continuous tradition over several centuries and embodying essential truths which are archaeologically verifiable. For example, the written accounts are correct for the settlement of Iceland: it was rapidly inhabited after 870 by people from Norway, Britain and Ireland, with several hundred large estates owned by chieftains and some 3,000 farms. The date can be verified from the 'settlement layer' of volcanic ash that covered a large part of the country following an eruption in about 871, which is corroborated by ice-core samples from the Greenland glacier, and immediately above this layer of ash are relics of the oldest settlements in Iceland. The saga writers and chroniclers also knew that people left Iceland to settle in Greenland near the end of the tenth century. Likewise they knew stories about sailings to the continent of North America around the turn of the millennium and they knew that heathendom was the prevailing faith during the settlement of Iceland, and that Christianity was adopted by law around 1000. Inconsistencies in detail, however, do not alter the overall picture which is presented and is well compatible with archaeological findings.

In recent decades one of the most important things that we have learned about oral tradition is that many of the basic assumptions made by earlier scholars about the nature of oral tradition were wrong. And if all these assumptions were wrong, we are bound to arrive at the conclusion that everything that has been based on them will have to be revised. We must therefore start again to work our way through the sources in order to determine if and how they might affect our interpretation of history and individual texts.

And here, the *Vinland Sagas* are a prime example. They were the victims of a scholarly methodology that led to the conclusion that *The Saga of the Greenlanders* was older and more reliable than *Eirik the Red's Saga*, which was claimed to have been written with the other as a source. This was the theory upon which Helge Ingstad operated when he found L'Anse aux Meadows in Newfoundland in the early 1960s.

Then the Icelandic scholar Ólafur Halldórsson[9] scrutinized the evidence, and came to the conclusion that verbal similarities between the two texts are not the result of literary borrowings or a written link. We must therefore assume that they were written down independently of one another, drawing on the same or similar traditional material that was circulating in oral tradition. Here we can therefore say that all the earlier scholarship, which was based on false assumptions about the nature of oral tradition and the textual relationship between the two sagas, must be discarded.

Icelandic sources give two versions of Eirik the Red's background. In the oldest, Ari the Learned's *Book of the Icelanders*, he is said to be 'a man from Breidafjord',[10] which is Ari's customary way of describing people who are born in Iceland. (He identifies people from Norway differently.) In later sources, *The Book of Settlements* and the sagas in which he appears, Eirik the Red is said to have hailed from Jaeren in Norway and gone to Iceland with his father. They lived first at Drangar on Hornstrandir, after which Eirik moved to Dalir in the Breidafjord area, where he married Thjodhild, daughter of Jorund. Her paternal great-grandmother was Rafarta, daughter of King Kjarval of Ireland. Thus Leif the Lucky, Eirik and Thjodhild's son, had Irish blood like so many others in the Dalir region. Eirik seems to have had a nose for trouble, as he was soon driven out of his district and eventually outlawed (see Glossary). During his exile he explored a land which he had heard of to the west of Iceland, and returned with news about 'Greenland', as he named it to attract others to join him in settling there. This is said to have happened fourteen or fifteen years before Christianity was adopted by law in Iceland, i.e. in 985 or 986.

Written sources make no mention of where and when Leif Eiriksson the Lucky was born, but given that his family moved to Greenland in 985 (or 986), after Eirik the Red returned from his three years of exploration there, it has been assumed that Leif was born in Eiriksstadir in Haukadal, Iceland, in order to be old enough to command a ship which sailed to the Hebrides (where he fathered a son), then to Norway and back to Greenland in 999–1000.

VOYAGES TO VINLAND IN THE SAGAS

When it comes to the Vinland voyages themselves, the sagas give two versions – which can nevertheless be matched in many instances (highlighted in bold on pp. xx–xxv). Comparison shows that their similarities are more striking than their contradictions, most of which can be explained by the oral traditions behind them. By collating them a reasonable sequence of events can be established, beginning in 999 and continuing until about 1006–1011, depending on which saga is preferred and how certain details are interpreted (see also the drawings pp. 63–64 of the 'mental maps' that can be extracted from the sagas about the respective locations of the mentioned sites and routes described):

1. Bjarni Herjolfsson sights unknown lands to the south and west of Greenland.
2. Leif the Lucky, son of Eirik the Red, becomes the first European to explore these lands and give names to locations, from north to south.
3. Thorvald, son of Eirik the Red, leads an expedition to Vinland.
4. Thorstein, son of Eirik the Red, tries to find Vinland but fails

and dies in Lysufjord, leaving Gudrid Thorbjarnardottir as a widow.

5. Thorfinn Karlsefni and Gudrid Thorbjarnardottir lead the first attempt to settle in the New World, during which they have the first European child born in America, Snorri.

6. Freydis, daughter of Eirik the Red, leads a disastrous expedition.

7. Thorfinn Karlsefni and Gudrid Thorbjarnardottir die in Skagafjord, Iceland.

EIRIK THE RED'S SAGA

Gudrid arrives in Greenland

Gudrid arrives in Greenland with her father in a group of 30 people who leave Iceland. Half of them fall sick and die on the way, but the rest are rescued. A seeress tells Gudrid's fortune, and she goes to Eirik the Red's residence.

Leif is instructed by King Olaf of Norway to convert Greenland to Christianity.

Leif finds new lands

Leif is blown off course and finds unknown land to the west of Greenland where self-sown wheat, grapes and burl wood grow. He rescues some people who have been shipwrecked and is given the nickname 'Lucky'.

Thorstein is lost in the Atlantic

Thorstein, Eirik's son, gets a ship from Gudrid's father and talks Eirik into coming along. He hides his gold before he leaves, then falls off his horse on the way to the ship and refuses to go. The others sail around in the Atlantic for the whole summer.

THE SAGA OF THE GREENLANDERS

Bjarni finds new lands

Bjarni Herjolfsson is blown off course and sees unknown, forested land west from Greenland.

Leif explores new lands and rescues Gudrid

Leif buys Bjarni's ship and asks **Eirik** to come along, but he claims to be too old and not accustomed to sailing any more. He finally agrees but falls off a horse on the way to the ship and returns to his farm without going anywhere.

Leif finds **Helluland, Markland and Vinland** and on his way back he **rescues Thorir** and his **crew, who are shipwrecked on a skerry, 15 people in all.** They all get sick the following winter and Thorir and many others die. **Gudrid** is Thorir's wife. **Leif is nicknamed 'the Lucky'** after rescuing these people.

Thorvald explores lands and dies on Krossanes

Thorvald, Leif's brother, explores west and east from Leif's camp and eventually **breaks his ship on a peninsula, Keel Point.**

He says he wants to settle nearby, but then they see nine men under three hide-covered boats and they kill all but one, who escapes. They are attacked by a huge number of natives who eventually withdraw. **Thorvald is fatally wounded by an arrow** and is buried on a point of land called Krossanes.

EIRIK THE RED'S SAGA

Thorstein and Gudrid are married

Thorstein marries Gudrid and they settle down in Lysufjord in the western settlement of Greenland. Thorstein falls ill, and dies but tells Gudrid's fortune. His remains are taken to consecrated ground in Brattahlid. Gudrid's father dies and she lives as a widow at Brattahlid.

Karlsefni and Gudrid's voyage

Thorfinn Karlsefni arrives in Greenland and marries Gudrid. There is much talk about going to Vinland and Karlsefni and Gudrid decide to set off, with Eirik's daughter Freydis and her husband Thorvard, and Eirik's son Thorvald. They find Helluland, Markland and Bjarney as well as a keel from a ship at Keel Point.

Stay in Stream Fjord

They pass Furdustrandir (Wonder beaches) and stay in Stream Fjord where they find a beached whale. One ship goes north around Keel Point in search of Vinland but is blown off course. Karlsefni continues south to Hop, taking his own livestock with him.

Meeting and battle with natives in Hop

Here they meet the natives (Skraelings) and Karlsefni and his men trade with them, selling them red cloth for pieces of skin. Karlsefni prevents his men from selling their weapons. A bull eventually scares the natives away.

The natives fight Karlsefni and his men – they flee, but the pregnant Freydis scares the natives away by baring her breasts. The natives find a dead man with an iron axe in his head, pick up the axe and try it successfully on wood, but when it breaks on stone they throw it away.

On his way back, Karlsefni kills five natives who are sleeping in skin sacks and who feed on blood and marrow.

THE SAGA OF THE GREENLANDERS

Thorstein and Gudrid marry and are lost at sea

Thorstein Eiriksson marries Gudrid, Thorir's widow, and they set out for Vinland but go astray at sea and end up in Lysufjord, where Thorstein dies but tells Gudrid's fortune. His remains are taken to consecrated ground in Brattahlid. Gudrid goes to Brattahlid.

Karlsefni and Gudrid's voyage

Thorfinn Karlsefni arrives in Greenland and marries Gudrid. There is much talk about going to Vinland and Karlsefni and Gudrid decide to go, intending to settle since they take livestock over with them.

Stay in Leif's camp

They reach Leif's camp where there is plenty of fresh beached whale, and they also live from the land, collect grapes and hunt.

Meeting and battle with natives

After one winter they become aware of natives, who turn out to be afraid of Karlsefni's bull. They trade with the natives who offer furs and want weapons in exchange, which Karlsefni forbids. Gudrid gives birth to Snorri and sees a phantom. Karlsefni plans to use their bull to scare off the natives. They attack, many natives die and one of them tries an iron axe on one of his companions, killing him. Their chief picks it up and throws it into the sea.

The following spring Karlsefni decides to return to Greenland, taking plenty of wood, berries and skins with him.

EIRIK THE RED'S SAGA

Thorvald dies in the Land of the One-Legged

Karlsefni sails around Keel Point and reaches a river where a uniped appears and shoots an arrow at Thorvald, Eirik the Red's son. He draws it out and admires the fat that is on it, a sign of well being and a fertile land.

They find out that they are looking at the other side of the same mountains they could see from Hop, with both places equidistant from Stream Fjord.

Snorri in Stream Fjord

Back in Stream Fjord, they begin to quarrel about women. Snorri, son of Gudrid and Karlsefni, is three years old. They take hostages on the way back and lose yet another ship.

Karlsefni and Gudrid in Skagafjord

Karlsefni and Gudrid settle on Reynines in Skagafjord. His mother dislikes Gudrid (because she feels Gudrid's family is not a good match for Karlsefni's) but accepts her in the end.

Three bishops are counted among their descendants.

THE SAGA OF THE GREENLANDERS

Freydis leads a voyage

Freydis Eiriksdottir leads a voyage with her husband, **Thorvard** from Gardar. The members of the expedition end up **fighting among themselves** in Leif's camp, incited by Freydis. She kills the women and her companions all go back to Greenland, where Freydis is condemned by Leif.

Karlsefni and Gudrid in Skagafjord

Karlsefni goes to Norway and sells his goods before returning to Glaumbaer in **Skagafjord,** where he and Gudrid settle down with their son **Snorri.** She goes on a pilgrimage, builds a church and becomes a nun.

Three bishops are counted among their descendants.

VINLAND VOYAGES IN ARCHAEOLOGY

In addition to the fairly detailed and realistic accounts of the Vinland voyages, there are the remains of buildings at L'Anse aux Meadows in Newfoundland, which were discovered in the early 1960s by Helge and Anna Ingstad. These buildings were of the same character as Viking Age buildings in Iceland and Greenland, and thus provided the first concrete proof of Scandinavian visitors to North America and hard evidence of at least one place they had visited. When Helge Ingstad in 1985 somewhat speculatively identified the site with Leif Eiriksson's Vinland as described in the sagas, this was based on the old assumption that *Eirik the Red's Saga* was a reworking of *The Saga of the Greenlanders*. This allowed him to reject some of the material found in *Eirik the Red's Saga* in favour of the accounts in *The Saga of the Greenlanders*, in which all the voyagers after Leif call at 'Leif's Camp'. Ingstad thus felt confident that he had discovered the one true Vinland. However, from archaeological work carried out since the early findings, it is now clear that L'Anse aux Meadows was in fact used as a staging post at an easily located point on the sea route from Greenland to lands farther south. Another advantage of the site was that it was not occupied by indigenous peoples, although northern Newfoundland had been occupied previously and would be again later; but around 1000 it was temporarily deserted.[11]

The site contained three dwelling halls and a number of smaller buildings which were used for only a few years around 1000 and would have housed 60–90 occupants. Both the largest and smallest halls contained large amounts of storage space. We can thus conclude that L'Anse aux Meadows was used as a wintering site, where ships could be pulled up on land for repairs and where goods were stockpiled. Kevin Smith has reported on nine pieces of jasper found among the Viking remains[12] – such stones were in common use for lighting fires by striking sparks against steel. Chemical analysis has shown that four of the stones probably came from the Qaarusuk region near to the Nordic Western Settlement in Greenland, while the other five most closely resemble jasper found in Borgarfjord and Hvalfjord in western Iceland.

A further pointer to the origins and cultural contacts of the people at L'Anse aux Meadows is a ringed pin of a type associated with Viking Dublin. Fastenings of this particular type are unknown from Norway but common in Viking Age finds from Ireland, Britain and Denmark, and fifteen have been found in Iceland. Other finds include ships' rivets, evidence of repair work, and a bone needle and a soapstone spindle whorl, indicating that there were women in the camp. These artefacts reinforce the picture of the voyagers in the Vinland sagas, namely that they included men and women from Iceland and Greenland with strong connections with the British Isles.

These travellers would in all probability have continued their journeys south into the Gulf of St Lawrence, rather than north around the tip of Newfoundland and then south along the dangerous and confusing east coast of the mainland. Also, the southern side of the gulf was the habitat of a sought-after plant species of which traces have been found at the camp: three butternuts (*Juglans cineria*) and a lump of burl wood from the butternut tree, with marks caused by an iron implement. Burl wood is particularly well suited to carving, and the use of iron tools is clear evidence that the marks were not made by Native Americans. The evidence also strongly suggests that the butternuts were brought to L'Anse aux Meadows by the people from Iceland and Greenland who used the place. They are not native to Newfoundland, their northernmost limit being on the southern side of the Gulf of St Lawrence, coinciding closely with the northernmost limit of wild grapes;[13] they were found in a pile of wood shavings from the Nordic occupation; they are too heavy to have been carried by birds and do not float, so must have been brought by people. The northern tip of Newfoundland would hardly give rise to memories about a land of wine and grapes, and the archaeological evidence confirms that the people who used L'Anse aux Meadows were also familiar with regions further south. There is thus absolutely no reason to identify the site with Vinland, as Ingstad attempted to do. However, it is highly unlikely that such a large staging post would have disappeared entirely from people's memories and it may well be that L'Anse aux Meadows is the place described in *The Saga of the Greenlanders*' accounts of the voyages of Thorvald (and Freydis).

Ever since the Vinland fascination took off in earnest in the first half of the nineteenth century, there have been numerous claims of discoveries of runic inscriptions and archaeological finds supposedly supporting particular theories of the location of Vinland and other places mentioned in the sagas. However, they have been shown with absolute certainty either to be hoaxes or to have no connections whatsoever with Viking Age Norsemen.[14] The only hitherto accepted candidate for a North American Viking Age relic from south of L'Anse aux Meadows is a coin found in 1957 at a Native American archaeological site in Maine. The coin was issued during the reign of Olaf the Peaceful, King of Norway (1067–93), and it was proposed that it perhaps came from the purse of the Bishop of Greenland, Eirik Upsi Gnupsson, who is said in the Icelandic annals for 1121 to have set out to look for Vinland himself but nothing more was ever heard of him or his ill-fated journey. A more likely possibility is that the coin was acquired farther north by indigenous peoples in contact with Icelandic Greenlanders and came south through trade or barter.[15] (However, even the authenticity of this coin has been cast in serious doubt by Edmund Carpenter.[16])

OTHER SOURCES ABOUT VINLAND

The earliest written reference to Vinland occurs in Adam of Bremen's *History of the Archbishops of Hamburg* from around 1075. He cites information that he received in 1068 or 1069 from the Danish king Svein Ulfsson about an island in the west named Vinland where there were both grapes and self-propagating wheat. Were it not for the *Vinland Sagas*, one would be tempted to suppose that Adam's description was of the marvellous legendary western islands.

A much briefer reference is found in Ari the Learned's *Book of the Icelanders*. He tells us that in Greenland Eirik the Red found evidence of 'human habitation' that indicated that the people who had lived there were of a similar kind to those who lived in Vinland and whom the Greenlanders called 'Skraelings'. Ari cites an unimpeachable source, namely his paternal uncle Thorkel Gellisson, who had been to Greenland and met there a man who 'himself had gone thither with Eirik the Red'.[17] Moreover, Ari's wording suggests that he assumed the existence of Vinland to be a generally known fact; indeed, one of the two bishops to whom he submitted his work for approval, Thorlak Runolfsson, Bishop of Skalholt (1085–1133), was the grandson of Snorri, and a man as likely as anyone to have known about the Vinland voyages. This all fits in well with the entry about Eirik Upsi Gnupsson, whose fateful journey in itself provides a further indication of a general awareness of Vinland and the earlier voyages across the Atlantic around the time that Ari was writing.

These references, as well as the sagas themselves, are absolutely clear about the meaning of 'wine' or 'grapes' in the name of 'Vínland' – i.e. *vín* rather than *vin*, which may possibly mean grass or meadow (a hypothesis evoked by Ingstad in order to argue for L'Anse aux Meadows as the Vinland). Assuming that the grapes are true wild grapes (*Vitis riparia*), and not just some kind of berry, they can be used to narrow down the search for Vinland. The northern limit can be set at the southern shores of the Gulf of St Lawrence, which almost forms an inland sea. Wild grapes were such a conspicuous part of the local flora in that area when the first post-Viking Europeans arrived in the sixteenth century that the French explorer Jacques Cartier (1491–1557) gave the name Île de Bacchus to a site near the modern city of Quebec, at the mouth of the St Lawrence. On the south side of Miramichi Bay in New Brunswick is a smaller bay called Baie de Vin (Wine Bay), a name which goes back to the early settlers. It is hardly possible to imagine anything closer in spirit to the way Leif regarded the land he visited 500 years earlier when he chose to call it Vinland. In spite of their literary and religious overtones in the sagas the grapes may therefore well have been real.

WHERE WAS VINLAND?

The northernmost states of New England were a favourite proposed location for Vinland in the nineteenth century and early in the twentieth century, whereas others have wanted to confine most of the descriptions to Newfoundland, the southern Gulf of St Lawrence and Nova Scotia. Even though very contradictory results seem to be suggested from analysing the same sources, it should be borne in mind that we are dealing not mainly with different interpretations of the saga texts but with different ideas about their nature, the textual relation between them and thus their reliability. Scholars have had opposing views which in turn have affected their reading of the texts. When there is contradictory information in the sagas between navigational directions and information about vegetation and climate, many have also been tempted to rely more on the descriptions of the land quality (such as the warm winter experienced by Leif in Vinland) rather than the sailing directions. It is fair to assume that the people who first told stories about the voyages to Vinland were skilled and experienced seafarers and that it was thus important to them to give and receive accurate information about the route, the length of the journey and landmarks. Such details were in all probability integrated into narratives about sea journeys, as is general practice among traditional oral societies that use stories and poems as a way of preserving knowledge. The basic message that the *Vinland Sagas* deliver is that Vinland is too dangerous to visit, because only one of the three ships from Karlsefni and Gudrid's expedition returned. Further, there are too many native inhabitants to make it a safe place for outsiders to settle, the route is long and a large group of men will have trouble in withstanding conditions so far from home, especially when few women are among the crew. Disputes tend to escalate under such conditions and can end in disaster, as Freydis's journey illustrates. The account of Thorvald's voyage and explorations from Leif's camp shows that the sailing route west of the camp was more favourable with shallow waters, and it specifically warns about the east coast route and the perils it entails, as shown by the fate of Thorvald's ship off Keel Point.

If we read the *Vinland Sagas* with the social role of stories about the voyages in mind and take the sagas seriously as sources, analysing carefully what they have to say about land-falls, bearings and sailing routes, and if, where they differ, we favour the fuller account over the shorter one, it becomes possible to build up a reasonably coherent mental map of the voyages undertaken. The fundamental methodological difference inherent in viewing these texts as the product of an oral tradition – rather than as historical documents of uneven reliability, or as works of literature to be analysed first and foremost in the light of the literary tradition and world view of the European Middle Ages – is that it allows us to put the two sagas together and consider the overall picture they present of the lands and sea routes to the south and west of Greenland, i.e. to make a whole and inclusive picture. We can suppose that this bears some resemblance to the image that thirteenth-century Icelanders might have built up in their own minds as they listened to the tales about the ancient voyages to Vinland: they had never been to these places themselves and they had no maps to put beside the descriptions of the routes taken, but these lands existed and they could visualize them in their mind's eye. This is the picture we need to try to re-create before considering whether and how well it corresponds with modern maps.

The details were, of course, not recorded as if they were entries in a ship's logbook. The first audiences did not have the knowledge or interest to deal with the descriptions, and the stories were repeated over the years by other storytellers to other audiences. But tellers and listeners would have constructed a mental image of their own of the configuration of the lands, an image good enough to provide a meaningful context.

When we try to interpret the saga texts it must not be assumed that everything has to fit what is known from L'Anse aux Meadows. Neither must one pay too much attention to what is likely to have been a regular sailing route for people from Greenland and Iceland to North America with Viking Age navigational techniques – once the area had been explored. Before these people had found out what was the most convenient route and which places could be frequented without running the risk of meeting too many hostile natives they can theoretically have gone far and wide because the sagas tell us that they spent several years on each voyage. And if they had a whole summer to sail south from the northernmost tip of Newfoundland, their curiosity cannot have been satisfied after just one day's sailing along its east and west coasts and the south coast of Labrador. It is more likely that these voyages took them much farther afield, especially in the light of what we know of the early exploration of both Iceland and Greenland.

We know that Eirik the Red spent three years exploring Greenland from south to north and covered it so well that he chose for himself the absolutely best farming area in this vast country. The same applies to accounts of early exploration in Iceland. The first explorers spent years and sailed all around the country, testing the conditions at various places to both north and south – Iceland is about 500 kilometres (310 miles) from east to west, comparable in size to Newfoundland from north to south or Nova Scotia from north-east to south-west. It was not until after several such voyages that the first settler, Ingolf Arnarson, arrived. And even he is said to have spent first one and then three years exploring some 400 kilometres (250 miles) of the south coast before eventually settling in Reykjavík – again an ideal location from his perspective in view of the entire region which he had gone through. This tells us that the seafarers were willing to build new winter camps for temporary purposes and to spend several years exploring new territories before they decided where to settle.

We can show that one sequence of events is more likely than another, as are some real locations. It is clear that the sagas are drawing on similar and comparable memories about the same voyages but that they are not equally well informed about them, and in that sense they complement each other. *The Saga of the Greenlanders* knows more about Leif and Thorvald, whereas *Eirik the Red's Saga* is better informed about Karlsefni. As a result *The Saga of the Greenlanders* sends Karlsefni to the same site as Thorvald went to earlier, throwing in grapes for good measure, but not really having anything to tell about him there. We should not interpret the account of Karlsefni's voyage in *Eirik the Red's Saga* as suggesting that its writer was compressing all three voyages of *The Saga of the Greenlanders* into one because he didn't know any better. The writer of *Eirik the Red's Saga* assumes his audience is familiar with previous voyages. A clear indication of this is that the notion of Keel Point and of the whereabouts of Leif's Vinland from *The Saga of the Greenlanders* is alive in *Eirik the Red's Saga* and the text of the latter makes it clear that Karlsefni and his crew do not go to Leif's Vinland but to a fjord with strong currents east of it and south from Keel Point. As Leif's Vinland is described as near or on an island north of the mainland, after two days' sailing over open water south-west from Markland, a picture begins to emerge:

Relative positions of the chief places named in the Vinland Sagas

Leif's *Vinland*	On or near an island that lies north of a shallow strait separating it from the mainland; two days' (*dœgr*) sailing south-west of *Markland*; west of *Keel Point*.
Leif's *Camp* in Thorvald's expedition	On land with islands and shallows to the west, where there are *white beaches*; dangerous waters when sailing north round the coast and then south on the eastern side.
Keel Point in Thorvald's and Karlsefni/Gudrid's expeditions	On a headland projecting north, south of *Leif's Camp*, east of Leif's *Vinland* and north of *Stream Fjord*. There are fjords on the eastern side of the land where *Keel Point* is – with an outreaching cape.
Wonder Beaches	On the way from *Keel Point* to *Stream Fjord*.
Stream Fjord	South of *Keel Point* and north of *Hop*.

| Hop ('Lagoon', 'Tidal Pool') | South of *Stream Fjord*. Between *Hop* and *Stream Fjord* there is a headland teeming with animals. |
| *Land of the One-Legged* | Some distance west and south of *Keel Point*; to the west of the mountains that lie between it and *Hop*. |

These are of course all very general descriptions, but they nevertheless fit the real places fairly well and form a relatively coherent picture if Leif's Vinland was in the Gulf of St Lawrence and if Karlsefni and Gudrid ventured south along the eastern coast of Nova Scotia, possibly as far south as the Bay of Fundy and perhaps even farther. The bay can rightly be called a Fjord of Streams as it has one of the most measured tidal differences (15–16 metres on average) on earth.

It is clear that the description in *The Saga of the Greenlanders* of the qualities of Vinland, as well as the island and the strait explored by Leif, cannot possibly be made to fit L'Anse aux Meadows. Leif's Camp in later expeditions cannot refer both to Leif's Vinland and to L'Anse aux Meadows, but there is the possibility that he stayed in places other than the one described in detail.

If we look more closely at the description of Leif's voyage in *The Saga of the Greenlanders*, we find fairly straightforward directions which can be used to navigate a Viking ship from Newfoundland across the Gulf of St Lawrence to Prince Edward Island and into the Northumberland Strait. They first go ashore on the island and taste the honey dew, but after they have entered the strait it is not clear whether they are supposed to go ashore on the island again or on the mainland. The saga therefore leaves open the possibility for the description to fit Prince Edward Island and the Miramichi Bay on the coast of New Brunswick, on the western side of the strait. There all the Vinland delicacies are to be found, but not the mild winter referred to in the saga, the only misfit in these descriptions.

It then is possible to explain the directions given in *Eirik the Red's Saga* about Karlsefni's voyage when he and his crew sail north from their Stream Fjord in order to round Keel Point and then turn west with land on their port side in order to find Leif's Vinland. These descriptions make sense if Stream Fjord was located in the southern regions of Nova Scotia. How far south from here Karlsefni may have gone is impossible to tell with certainty but reasonable suggestions have been made for the coast of New England, and even as far as New York. However, these northerners would have experienced different waters which required different navigational techniques from those they were used to. The reference to mountains which they observe from the other side after a long sailing north and west (to the Gulf of St Lawrence?) could be an indication that they were aware of the Appalachian Mountains, and the headland on the way north from Hop recalls the only prominent headland between the Bay of Fundy and New York, namely Cape Cod.

The self-propagating wheat mentioned in the sagas may refer to wild rye (*Elymus virginicus*), which grows in the same area as the grapes and looks much like wheat.[18] The northern limits of both wild rye and wild grapes coincide fairly closely with the northern limit of the butternut, showing that the explorers who brought these nuts to L'Anse aux Meadows would also have come across true wild grapes in profusion on their travels.

According to *The Saga of the Greenlanders*, Leif and his men encountered salmon in Vinland, both larger and more numerous than any they had seen before. The Canadian archaeologist Catherine Carlson[19] has shown that in the eleventh century there were no salmon as far south as the rivers of Maine, because of the warmer climate then prevailing. The rivers flowing into the southern shores of the Gulf of St Lawrence, however, would have been, then as now, teeming with salmon.

Putting all this together, the likely location of Leif's Vinland can be narrowed down to Prince Edward Island and the southern shores of the Gulf of St Lawrence. The name Vinland is also used about the location reached by Karlsefni and Gudrid, showing us that Vinland in the sagas can be viewed as reaching further south. Other natural resources mentioned in the sagas also point to this: for instance, the burl wood, which grows on several types of tree from the Gulf to New England, and the beached whale. Slightly more problematic are the 'holy fish'

(*helgir fiskar*) caught by Karlsefni at Hop. This certainly refers
to some kind of flatfish: the term is often translated 'halibut',
though in fact the species is unclear. The latest and most ex-
haustive attempt to identify this fish has been made by Páll
Bergþórsson,[20] who believes it to have been the winter flounder
(*Pseudopleuronectes americanus*), which is common in these
southerly waters. Karlsefni's Hop lay well to the south of Leif's
Vinland and the sources mention good catches of fish, but,
perhaps significantly, not salmon, which might point to Hop
having been beyond the southern limit of salmon distribution.

Owing to the fact that the sagas are written down from oral
accounts many generations after the actual events took place,
they cannot be used to prove the exact location of the sites that
they describe. In spite of this the overall picture that emerges is
reasonably clear: around the year 1000 people from Greenland
and Iceland went on several voyages along the eastern coast of
North America, into the Gulf of St Lawrence and further south.
They built camps in more than one location and spent a winter
or several years in them. They came into contact with natives,
sometimes on friendly terms as traders, but also fought battles
against them. Internal conflicts among themselves as well as
attacks from the natives eventually led to their departure. After
that it is unlikely that the Greenlanders went as far south as the
saga men had, but it is highly probable that they went to
Labrador on a regular basis to get wood, all through the Middle
Ages – as we have a casual reference in an Icelandic chronicle
for 1347 to such a trip, which seems to be regarded as common
practice.

Many lived to tell of these early adventures in Iceland, and
writers later composed the sagas which are now our major
source on the first documented European voyage to America.
We have found physical remains from their stay in L'Anse aux
Meadows, and where do you go from there if you have a whole
summer ahead of you to explore new lands and gather goods
to take back home to Greenland? You go south and into the
Gulf of St Lawrence, to hunt for the fruits and vegetation that
Greenland lacks. You may even try to settle, only to find the
land already crowded[21] with native people, so you end up going

back home and devoting the rest of your life to boasting of the
great time you and your crew had when you spent the summers
sailing across the seven seas and discovering new and previously
unheard-of lands . . . just as the sagas tell us.

Gísli Sigurðsson

NOTES

1. Ólafur Halldórsson (ed.), *Eiríks saga rauða*, Íslenzk fornrit 4
   (supplement) (Reykjavík, 1985), p. 368.
2. *The Saga of the People of Laxardal*, trans. Keneva Kunz and ed.
   Bergljót S. Kristjánsdóttir (London, 2008).
3. Ólafur Halldórsson, 'Á afmæli Flateyjarbókar', *Grettisfærsla*
   (Reykjavík, 1990), p. 208.
4. Helgi Þorláksson, 'The Vínland Sagas in a Contemporary Light',
   in *Approaches to Vínland*, ed. Andrew Wawn and Þórunn Sigurðardóttir (Reykjavík, 2001), pp. 63–77.
5. Hermann Pálsson, 'Vínland Revisited', *Northern Studies*, 35
   (2000), pp. 11–38, and *Vínlandið góða og írskar ritningar*
   (Reykjavík, 2001).
6. Theodore M. Andersson, 'Exoticism in Early Iceland', in *International Scandinavian and Medieval Studies in Memory of Gerd
   Wolfgang Weber*, ed. Michael Dallapiazza et al. (Trieste, 2000),
   pp. 19–28.
7. *The Complete Sagas of Icelanders*, ed. Viðar Hreinsson (Reykjavík, 1997).
8. See Birgitta Wallace and William W. Fitzhugh, 'Stumbles and
   Pitfalls in the Search for Viking America', in *Vikings: The North
   Atlantic Saga*, ed. William W. Fitzhugh and Elisabeth I. Ward
   (Washington, DC, and London, 2000), pp. 374–84. See also
   Kirsten A. Seaver, *Maps, Myths, and Men: The Story of the
   Vínland Map* (Stanford, CA, 2004).
9. Halldórsson's conclusions on this matter (in his *Grænland í
   miðaldaritum* (Reykjavík, 1978), conveniently summarized in
   Eiríks saga rauða, ed. Halldórsson) have not been challenged and
   are now generally accepted, see Vésteinn Ólason, 'Saga-tekstene
   – forskningsstatus', in *Leif Eiriksson, Helge Ingstad og Vinland*,
   ed. Jan Ragnar Hagland and Steinar Supphellen (Trondheim,
   2001), pp. 41–64.

10. *Íslendingabók (The Book of the Icelanders)*, trans. Halldór Hermannson (Ithaca, NY, 1930), p. 64.

11. Birgitta Wallace, 'The Viking Settlement at L'Anse aux Meadows', in *Vikings: The North Atlantic Saga*, ed. Fitzhugh and Ward, pp. 208–16.

12. Kevin Smith, 'Who Lived at L'Anse aux Meadows?', in *Vikings: The North Atlantic Saga*, ed. Fitzhugh and Ward, p. 217.

13. Wallace, 'The Viking Settlement at L'Anse aux Meadows', p. 216.

14. See Wallace and Fitzhugh, 'Stumbles and Pitfalls in the Search for Viking America'.

15. Steven L. Cox, 'A Norse Penny from Maine', in *Vikings: The North Atlantic Saga*, ed. Fitzhugh and Ward, pp. 206–7.

16. Edmund Carpenter, *Norse Penny* (New York, 2003).

17. *Íslendingabók*, trans. Hermannson, p. 64.

18. Mats G. Larsson, 'The Vinland Sagas and Nova Scotia: A Reappraisal of an Old Theory', *Scandinavian Studies*, 64:3 (1992), pp. 305–35.

19. Catherine Carlson, 'The (in)significance of Atlantic Salmon', *Federal Archaeology*, 8:3–4 (1996), pp. 22–30.

20. Páll Bergþórsson, *The Wineland Millennium: Saga and Evidence* (Reykjavík, 2000).

21. See Robert McGhee, *Canada Rediscovered* (Canadian Museum of Civilization, 1991), p. 50.

Further Reading

PRIMARY OLD ICELANDIC SOURCES IN TRANSLATION

The Book of Settlements, trans. Hermann Pálsson and Paul Edwards (Winnipeg, 1972).

The Complete Sagas of Icelanders, including 49 Tales, ed. Viðar Hreinsson, 5 vols. (Reykjavík, 1997).

Íslendingabók (The Book of the Icelanders), trans. Halldór Hermannson (Ithaca, NY, 1930).

Laws of Early Iceland: Grágás, trans. Andrew Dennis, Peter Foote and Richard Perkins, 2 vols. (Winnipeg, 1980, 2000).

Snorri Sturluson, *Edda [Prose Edda]*, trans. Anthony Faulkes (London, 1987).

Snorri Sturluson, *Heimskringla*, trans. Lee M. Hollander (Austin, TX, 1964).

Sturlunga Saga, trans. Julia McGrew and R. George Thomas (New York, 1970–74).

GENERAL

Andersson, Theodore M., *The Problem of Icelandic Saga Origins: A Historical Survey* (New Haven, CN, 1964).

Byock, Jesse L., *Viking Age Iceland* (London, 2001).

Clover, Carol J., and John Lindow (eds.), *Old Norse-Icelandic Literature: A Critical Guide*, Islandica 45 (Ithaca, NY, 1985).

Clunies Ross, Margaret (ed.), *Old Icelandic Literature and Society* (Cambridge, 2000).

Foote, Peter, and David M. Wilson, *The Viking Achievement* (London, 1970).

Jesch, Judith, *Women in the Viking Age* (Woodbridge, 1991).

Jochens, Jenny, *Old Norse Images of Women* (Philadelphia, 1996).

Jones, Gwyn, *A History of the Vikings* (Oxford and New York, 1984).

Kristjánsson, Jónas, *Eddas and Sagas: Iceland's Medieval Literature*, trans. Peter Foote (Reykjavík, 1992).

McTurk, Rory (ed.), *A Companion to Old Norse-Icelandic Literature and Culture* (Oxford, 2005).

Meulengracht Sørensen, Preben, *Saga and Society: An Introduction to Old Norse Literature*, trans. John Tucker (Odense, Denmark, 1993).

Miller, William Ian, *Bloodtaking and Peacemaking: Feud, Law, and Society in Saga Iceland* (Chicago, 1990).

Nordal, Guðrún, *Tools of Literacy: The Role of Skaldic Verse in Icelandic Textual Culture of the Twelfth and Thirteenth Centuries* (Toronto, 2001).

Ólason, Vésteinn, *Dialogues with the Viking Age: Narration and Representation in the Sagas of Icelanders*, trans. Andrew Wawn (Reykjavík, 1997).

Pulsiano, Phillip, et al. (eds.), *Medieval Scandinavia: An Encyclopedia* (New York, 1993).

Sigurðsson, Gísli, *Gaelic Influence in Iceland: Historical and Literary Contacts, A Survey of Research* (Reykjavík, 1988, 2000).

Steblin-Kamenskij, M. I., *The Saga Mind*, trans. Kenneth H. Ober (Odense, Denmark, 1973).

Tucker, John (ed.), *Sagas of the Icelanders* (New York, 1989).

Tulinius, Torfi H., *The Matter of the North: The Rise of Literary Fiction in Thirteenth-Century Iceland*, trans. Randi C. Eldevik (Odense, Denmark, 2002).

Turville-Petre, E. O. G., *Origins of Icelandic Literature* (Oxford, 1953).

VINLAND SAGAS

Agnarsdóttir, Anna (ed.), *Voyages and Exploration in the North Atlantic from the Middle Ages to the XVIIth Century* (Reykjavík, 2001).

Andersson, Theodore M., 'Exoticism in Early Iceland', in *International Scandinavian and Medieval Studies in Memory of Gerd Wolfgang Weber*, ed. Michael Dallapiazza et al. (Trieste, 2000), pp. 19–28.

Bergersen, Robert, *Vinland Bibliography: Writings relating to the Norse in Greenland and America* (Tromsø, Norway, 1997).

Bergþórsson, Páll, *The Wineland Millennium: Saga and Evidence* (Reykjavík, 2000).

Carlson, Catherine, 'The (in)significance of Atlantic Salmon', *Federal Archaeology*, 8:3–4 (1996), pp. 22–30.

Carpenter, Edmund, *Norse Penny* (New York, 2003).

Cartier, Jacques, *Relations*, ed. Michel Bideaux (Montreal, 1986).

Cox, Steven L., 'A Norse Penny from Maine', in *Vikings: The North Atlantic Saga*, ed. William W. Fitzhugh and Elisabeth I. Ward (Washington, DC, and London, 2000), pp. 206–7.

Halldórsson, Ólafur (ed.), *Eiríks saga rauða*, Íslenzk fornrit 4 (supplement) (Reykjavík, 1985).

—, *Grænland í miðaldaritum* (Reykjavík, 1978).

Hermannsson, Halldór, *The Problem of Wineland*, Islandica 25 (Ithaca, NY, 1936).

Ingstad, Helge, *The Norse Discovery of America* (Oslo, 1985), vol. 2.

Jones, Gwyn, *The Norse Atlantic Saga: Being the Norse Voyages of Discovery and Settlement to Iceland, Greenland and North America*, new and enlarged edn (Oxford and New York, 1986).

Krogh, Knud J., *Viking Greenland*, trans. Helen Fogh and Gwyn Jones (Copenhagen, 1967).

Larsson, Mats G., 'The Vinland Sagas and Nova Scotia: A

Reappraisal of an Old Theory', *Scandinavian Studies*, 64:3 (1992), pp. 305–35.

Lewis-Simpson, Shannon (ed.), *Vínland Revisited: The Norse World at the Turn of the First Millennium* (Québec, 2003).

Mortensen, Andras, and Símun V. Arge (eds.), *Viking and Norse in the North Atlantic* (Tórshavn, 2005).

Ólafsson, Guðmundur, *Eiríksstaðir í Haukadal* (Reykjavík, 1998).

Pálsson, Hermann, 'Vínland Revisited', *Northern Studies*, 35 (2000), pp. 11–38.

—, *Vínlandið góða og írskar ritningar* (Reykjavík, 2001).

Seaver, Kirsten A., *The Frozen Echo: Greenland and the Exploration of North America ca A.D. 1000–1500* (Stanford, CA 1996).

Sigurðsson, Gísli, *The Medieval Icelandic Saga and Oral Tradition: A Discourse on Method* (Cambridge, MA and London, 2004).

Smith, Kevin, 'Who Lived at L'Anse aux Meadows?', in *Vikings: The North Atlantic Saga*, ed. William W. Fitzhugh and Elisabeth I. Ward (Washington, DC, and London, 2000), p. 217.

Storm, Gustav, 'Om Betydningen av "Eyktarstaðr" i Flatøbogens Beretning om Vinlandsreiserne', *Arkiv för nordisk filologi*, 3 (1886), pp. 121–31.

—, 'Studier over Vinlandsreiserne, Vinlands geografi og ethnografi', in *Aarbøger for nordisk oldkyndighed og historie* (1887), pp. 293–372.

Wallace, Birgitta, 'The Viking Settlement at L'Anse aux Meadows', in *Vikings: The North Atlantic Saga*, ed. William W. Fitzhugh and Elisabeth I. Ward (Washington, DC, and London, 2000), pp. 208–16.

—, *Westward Vikings: The Saga of L'Anse aux Meadows* (St John's, 2006).

—, and William W. Fitzhugh, 'Stumbles and Pitfalls in the Search for Viking America', in *Vikings: The North Atlantic Saga*, ed. Fitzhugh and Ward, pp. 374–84.

Þorláksson, Helgi, 'The Vínland Sagas in a Contemporary Light', in *Approaches to Vínland*, ed. Andrew Wawn and Þórunn Sigurðardóttir (Reykjavík, 2001), pp. 63–77.

A Note on the Translation

The Saga of the Greenlanders is translated by Keneva Kunz from Ólafur Halldórsson's *Grænland í miðaldaritum* (Reykjavík, 1978).

Eirik the Red's Saga is translated by Keneva Kunz from the edition in the supplement to *Íslenzk fornrit 4* (Reykjavík, 1985), pp. 403–34, in which the philologist Ólafur Halldórsson has used the *Skálholtsbók* manuscript, which contains the better version of the saga. It often differs considerably from other editions where editors have chosen variant readings or used the *Hauksbók* text.

Both translations were originally published in *The Complete Sagas of Icelanders* (Leifur Eiríksson, 1997), and reprinted with minor revisions in *The Sagas of Icelanders* (Penguin, 2000), which is the version used for the present edition with a few further changes.

The translator's aim, and that of everyone engaged in the *Complete Sagas of Icelanders* project, has been above all to strike a balance between faithfulness to the original text and appeal to the modern reader. The *Complete Sagas* also sought to reflect the homogeneity of the world of the Sagas of Icelanders, by aiming for consistency in the translation of certain essential vocabulary, for instance terms relating to legal practices, social and religious practices, farm layouts or types of ships.

As is common in translations from Old Icelandic, the spelling of proper nouns has been simplified, both by the elimination of non-English letters and by the reduction of inflections. Thus 'Guðríður Þorbjarnardóttir' becomes 'Gudrid Thorbjarnardottir' and 'Leifur Eiríksson' becomes 'Leif Eiriksson'. The reader will soon grasp that '-dottir' means 'daughter of' and '-son' means 'son of'. Place names have been rendered in a similar way, often with an English identifier of the landscape feature in question (e.g. 'Hraunhafnaros estuary,' in which 'Hraunhaf-nar-' means 'lava harbour' and '-os' means 'estuary'). A translation is given in parentheses at the first occurrence of place names when the context requires this, such as Gunnbjarnarsker (Gunnbjorn's skerry). For place names outside Scandinavia, the common English equivalent is used if such exists; otherwise the Icelandic form has been transliterated. Nicknames are translated where their meanings are reasonably certain.

THE SAGA OF THE
GREENLANDERS

1 | Herjolf was the son of Bard Herjolfsson and a kinsman of Ingolf, the settler of Iceland.[1] Ingolf gave to Herjolf the land between Vog and Reykjanes.

At first, Herjolf farmed at Drepstokk. His wife was named Thorgerd and their son was Bjarni; he was a promising young man. While still a youthful age he longed to sail abroad. He soon earned himself both a good deal of wealth and a good name, and spent his winters alternately abroad and with his father. Soon Bjarni had his own ship making trading voyages. During the last winter Bjarni spent in Norway, Herjolf decided to accompany Eirik the Red to Greenland and left his farm. One of the men on Herjolf's ship was from the Hebrides, a Christian, who composed the drapa of the Sea Fences (Breakers).[2] It has this refrain:

I ask you, unblemished monks' tester,   *monk's tester:* Christ
to be the ward of my travels;
may the lord of the peaks' pane   *peaks' pane:* heavens
shade my path with his hawk's perch.   *hawk's perch:* hand

Herjolf farmed at Herjolfsnes (Herjolf's point). He was the most respected of men.

Eirik the Red farmed at Brattahlid. There he was held in the highest esteem, and everyone deferred to his authority. Eirik's children were Leif, Thorvald, Thorstein and a daughter, Freydis. She was married to a man named Thorvard, and they farmed at Gardar, where the bishop's seat is now. She was a

domineering woman, but Thorvard was a man of no conse-
quence. She had been married to him mainly for his money.

Heathen were the people of Greenland at that time.

Bjarni steered his ship into Eyrar in the summer of the year
that his father had sailed from Iceland. Bjarni was greatly
moved by the news and would not have his cargo unloaded.
His crew then asked what he was waiting for, and he answered
that he intended to follow his custom of spending the winter
with his father – 'and I want to set sail for Greenland, if you
will join me'.

All of them said they would follow his counsel.

Bjarni then spoke: 'Our journey will be thought an ill-
considered one, since none of us has sailed the Greenland Sea.'

Despite this they set sail once they had made ready and
sailed for three days, until the land had disappeared below the
horizon. Then the wind dropped and they were beset by winds
from the north and fog; for many days they did not know where
they were sailing.

After that they saw the sun and could take their bearings.
Hoisting the sail, they sailed for the rest of the day before
sighting land. They speculated among themselves as to what
land this would be, for Bjarni said he suspected this was not
Greenland.

They asked whether he wished to sail up close into the shore
of this country or not. 'My advice is that we sail in close to the
land.'

They did so, and soon saw that the land was not mountainous
but did have small hills, and was covered with forests. Keeping
it on their port side, they turned their sail-end landwards and
angled away from the shore.

They sailed for another two days before sighting land once
again.

They asked Bjarni whether he now thought this to be
Greenland.

He said he thought this no more likely to be Greenland than
the previous land – 'since there are said to be very large glaciers
in Greenland'.

They soon approached the land and saw that it was flat and

wooded. The wind died and the crew members said they thought it advisable to put ashore, but Bjarni was against it. They claimed they needed both timber and water.

'You've no shortage of those provisions,' Bjarni said, but he was criticized somewhat by his crew for this.

He told them to hoist the sail and they did so, turning the stern towards shore and sailing seawards. For three days they sailed with the wind from the south-west until they saw a third land. This land had high mountains, capped by a glacier.

They asked whether Bjarni wished to make land here, but he said he did not wish to do so – 'as this land seems to me to offer nothing of use'.[3]

This time they did not lower the sail, but followed the shore-line until they saw that the land was an island. Once more they turned their stern landwards and sailed out to sea with the same breeze. But the wind soon grew and Bjarni told them to lower the sail and not to proceed faster than both their ship and rigging could safely withstand. They sailed for four days.

Upon seeing a fourth land they asked Bjarni whether he thought this was Greenland or not.

Bjarni answered, 'This land is most like what I have been told of Greenland, and we'll head for shore here.'

This they did and made land along a headland in the evening of the day, finding a boat there. On this point Herjolf, Bjarni's father, lived, and it was named for him and has since been called Herjolfsnes. Bjarni now joined his father and ceased his merchant voyages. He remained on his father's farm as long as Herjolf lived and took over the farm after his death.

2 | Following this, Bjarni Herjolfsson sailed from Greenland to Earl Eirik,[4] who received him well. Bjarni told of his voyage, during which he had sighted various lands, and many people thought him short on curiosity, since he had nothing to tell of these lands, and he was criticized somewhat for this.

Bjarni became one of the earl's followers and sailed to Greenland the following summer. There was now much talk of looking for new lands.

Leif, the son of Eirik the Red of Brattahlid, sought out Bjarni and purchased his ship. He hired himself a crew numbering thirty-five men altogether. Leif asked his father Eirik to head the expedition.

Eirik was reluctant to agree, saying he was getting on in years and not as good at bearing the cold and wet as before. Leif said he still commanded the greatest good fortune of all his kinsmen. Eirik gave in to Leif's urgings and, when they were almost ready, set out from his farm on horseback. When he had but a short distance left to the ship, the horse he was riding stumbled and threw Eirik, injuring his foot. Eirik then spoke: 'I am not intended to find any other land than this one where we now live. This will be the end of our travelling together.'

Eirik returned home to Brattahlid, and Leif boarded his ship, along with his companions, thirty-five men altogether. One of the crew was a man named Tyrkir, from a more southerly country.[5]

Once they had made the ship ready, they put to sea and found first the land which Bjarni and his companions had seen last. They sailed up to the shore and cast anchor, put out a boat and rowed ashore. There they found no grass, but large glaciers covered the highlands, and the land was like a single flat slab of rock from the glaciers to the sea. This land seemed to them of little use.

Leif then spoke: 'As far as this land is concerned it can't be said of us as of Bjarni, that we did not set foot on shore. I am now going to name this land and call it Helluland (Stone-slab land).'

They then returned to their ship, put out to sea and found a second land. Once more they sailed close to the shore and cast anchor, put out a boat and went ashore. This land was flat and forested, sloping gently seaward, and they came across many beaches of white sand.

Leif then spoke: 'This land will be named for what it has to offer and called Markland (Forest land).'[6] They then returned to the ship without delay.

After this they sailed out to sea and spent two days at sea with a north-easterly wind before they saw land.[7] They sailed towards it and came to an island, which lay to the north of the land, where they went ashore. In the fine weather they found dew on the grass, that they collected in their hands and drank, and thought they had never tasted anything as sweet.

Afterwards they returned to their ship and sailed into the sound which lay between the island and the headland that stretched out northwards from the land. They rounded the headland and steered westward. Here there were extensive shallows at low tide and their ship was soon stranded, and the sea looked far away to those aboard ship.

Their curiosity to see the land was so great that they could not be bothered to wait for the tide to come in and float their stranded ship, and they ran aground where a river flowed into the sea from a lake. When the incoming tide floated the ship again, they took the boat and rowed to the ship and moved it up into the river and from there into the lake, where they cast anchor. They carried their sleeping-sacks ashore and built booths. Later they decided to spend the winter there and built large houses.

There was no lack of salmon both in the lake and in the river, and this salmon was larger than they had ever seen before.[8]

It seemed to them the land was so good that livestock would need no fodder during the winter. The temperature never dropped below freezing, and the grass only withered very slightly. The days and nights were much more equal in length than in Greenland or Iceland. In the depth of winter the sun was aloft by mid-morning and still visible at mid-afternoon.[9]

When they had finished building their houses, Leif spoke to his companions: 'I want to divide our company into two groups, as I wish to explore the land. One half is to remain at home by the longhouses while the other half explores the land. They are never to go any farther than will enable them to return that same evening and no one is to separate from the group.'

This they did for some time. Leif accompanied them sometimes, and at other times remained at home by the houses. Leif was a large, strong man, of very striking appearance and wise, as well as being a man of moderation in all things.

3 | One evening it happened that one man, the southerner
    Tyrkir, was missing from their company. Leif was very
upset by this, as Tyrkir had spent many years with him and his
father and had treated Leif as a child very affectionately. Leif
criticized his companions harshly and prepared to search for
Tyrkir, taking twelve men with him.

When they had gone only a short way from the houses, however, Tyrkir came towards him and they welcomed him gladly.

Leif soon realized that the companion of his childhood was
pleased about something. Tyrkir had a protruding forehead
and darting eyes, with dark wrinkles in his face; he was short
in stature and frail-looking, but a master of all types of crafts.

Leif then asked him, 'Why were you so late returning, foster-
father, and how did you become separated from the rest?'

For a long time Tyrkir only spoke in German, with his eyes
darting in all directions and his face contorted. The others
understood nothing of what he was saying.

After a while he spoke in Norse: 'I had gone only a bit farther
than the rest of you. But I have news to tell you: I found
grapevines and grapes.'[10]

'Are you really sure of this, foster-father?' Leif said.

'I'm absolutely sure,' he replied, 'because where I was born
there was no lack of grapevines and grapes.'

They went to sleep after that, and the following morning Leif
spoke to his crew: 'We'll divide our time between two tasks,
taking one day for one task and one day for the other, picking
grapes or cutting vines and felling the trees to make a load for
my ship.' They agreed on this course.

It is said that the boat which was drawn behind the ship was
filled with grapes.

Then they cut a load for the ship.

When spring came they made the ship ready and set sail. Leif
named the land for its natural features and called it Vinland
(Wineland).[11] They headed out to sea and had favourable
winds, until they came in sight of Greenland and the mountains
under its glaciers.

Then one of the crew spoke up, asking, 'Why do you steer a
course so close to the wind?'

Leif answered, 'I'm watching my course, but there's more to it than that: do you see anything of note?'

The crew said they saw nothing worthy of note.

'I'm not sure,' Leif said, 'whether it's a ship or a skerry that I see.'

They then saw it and said it was a skerry. Leif saw so much better than they did, that he could make out men on the skerry.

'I want to steer us close into the wind,' Leif said, 'so that we can reach them; if these men should be in need of our help, we have to try to give it to them. If they should prove to be hostile, we have all the advantages on our side and they have none.'

They managed to sail close to the skerry and lowered their sail, cast anchor and put out one of the two extra boats they had taken with them.

Leif then asked who was in charge of the company.

The man who replied said his name was Thorir and that he was of Norwegian origin. 'And what is your name?'

Leif told him his name.

'Are you the son of Eirik the Red of Brattahlid?' he asked.

Leif said he was. 'Now I want to invite all of you,' Leif said, 'to come on board my ship, bringing as much of your valuables as the ship can carry.'

After they had accepted his offer, the ship sailed to Eiriksfjord with all this cargo until they reached Brattahlid, where they unloaded the ship. Leif then invited Thorir to spend the winter with him there, along with Thorir's wife Gudrid and three other men, and found places for the other members of both his own and Thorir's crew. Leif rescued fifteen men from the skerry. After this he was called Leif the Lucky.

Leif had now become very wealthy and was held in much respect.

That winter Thorir's crew were stricken by illness and he himself died, along with most of his company. Eirik the Red also died that winter.

There was great discussion of Leif's Vinland voyage and his brother Thorvald felt they had not explored enough of the land. Leif then said to Thorvald, 'You go to Vinland, brother, and take my ship if you wish, but before you do so I want the ship to make a trip to the skerry to fetch the wood that Thorir had there.'

And so this was done.

4 | In consultation with his brother Leif, Thorvald now pre-
  | pared for this journey with thirty companions. They made
their ship ready and put to sea, and nothing is told of their
journey until they came to Vinland, to Leif's camp, where they
laid up their ship and settled in for the winter, fishing for their
food.

That spring Thorvald said they should make their ship ready
and several men were to take the ship's boat and go to the west
of the land and explore there during the summer. They thought
the land fine and well forested, with white beaches and only a
short distance between the forest and the sea. There were many
islands and wide stretches of shallow sea.

Nowhere did they see signs of men or animals. On one of
the westerly islands they did find a wooden grain cover, but
discovered no other work by human hands and headed back,
returning to Leif's camp in the autumn.

The second summer Thorvald explored the country to the
east on the large ship, going north around the land.[12] They ran
into stormy weather around one headland, and they were driven
ashore, smashing the keel of the ship. They stayed there a long
time, repairing their ship. Thorvald then said to his companions, 'I want us to raise the broken keel up on this point
and call it Kjalarnes (Keel point).'[13] This they did.

They then left to sail to the east of the country and entered
the mouths of the next fjords until they reached a cape stretching out seawards. It was covered with forest. After they secured
their ship in a sheltered cove and put out gangways to the land,
Thorvald and all his companions went ashore.

He then spoke: 'This is an attractive spot, and here I would
like to build my farm.' As they headed back to the ship they
saw three hillocks on the beach inland from the cape. Upon
coming closer they saw they were three hide-covered boats,
with three men under each of them. They divided their forces

and managed to capture all of them except one, who escaped with his boat. They killed the other eight and went back to the cape. On surveying the area they saw a number of hillocks further up the fjord, and assumed them to be settlements.

Following this they were stricken by sleep, so that they could no longer keep their eyes open, and all of them fell asleep. Then a voice was heard calling, and they all woke up. 'Wake up, Thorvald, and all your companions,' the voice warned, 'if you wish to save your lives. Get to the ship with all your men and leave this land as quickly as you can.'

A vast number of hide-covered boats came down the fjord, heading towards them.

Thorvald then spoke: 'We will set up breastworks along the sides of the ship and defend ourselves as well as possible, but fight back as little as we can.'

They did as he said, and after the natives[14] had shot at them for a while, they fled as rapidly as they could.

Thorvald then asked his men if they had been wounded, and they replied that they were unhurt.

'I have been wounded under my arm,' he said. 'An arrow flew between the edge of the ship and the shield into my armpit. Here is the arrow, and this wound will cause my death. I now advise you to prepare for your return journey as quickly as possible, but take me to that cape I thought was such a good farm site. Perhaps the words I spoke will prove true enough and I will dwell there awhile. You will bury me there and mark my grave with crosses at the head and foot, and call the spot Krossanes (Cross point) after that.'

Greenland had been converted to Christianity by that time, although Eirik the Red had died before the conversion.

Thorvald then died, and they did everything as he had advised, then left to meet up with their companions. Each group told its news to the other and they spent the winter there loading the ships with grapes and grapevines.

In the spring they made ready for the voyage back to Greenland. They steered the ship into Eiriksfjord and had plenty of news to tell Leif.

5 | Among the events taking place meanwhile in Greenland
    was the marriage of Thorstein Eiriksson to Gudrid
Thorbjarnardottir, who had previously been married to Thorir
the Norwegian who was spoken of earlier.

Thorstein Eiriksson now wished to sail to Vinland to retrieve
his brother Thorvald's body and made the same ship ready
once more. He selected his companions for their strength and
size, taking with him twenty-five men and his wife, Gudrid.
Once they had made ready, they set sail and were out of sight
of land. They were tossed about at sea all summer and did not
know where they were.

The first week of winter had passed when they made land in
Lysufjord, in the western settlement in Greenland. Thorstein
managed to find places for all his crew members. But he and
his wife had no accommodation and remained alone on the
ship for several nights. In those days Christianity was still in its
infancy in Greenland.

One day some men came to their tent early in the day. The
leader of the group asked what men were in the tent.

Thorstein answered, 'There are two of us,' he said, 'and who
is asking?'

'Thorstein is my name, and I am called Thorstein the Black.
My reason for coming is to invite you and your wife to stay the
winter with me.'

Thorstein Eiriksson said he wished to seek his wife's
guidance, and when she told him to decide he agreed to the
offer.

'Then I'll return with a team of oxen to fetch you tomorrow,
as I do not lack the means to put you up. But it will be an
unexciting stay, as there are only the two of us, my wife and
myself, and I prefer my own company. Also I have another
faith than you, although I expect yours is the better of the
two.'

He then came with a team of oxen to fetch them the next
day, and so they went to stay with Thorstein the Black, and he
provided for them generously.

Gudrid was a woman of striking appearance and wise as
well, who knew how to behave among strangers.

It was early in the winter when the first of Thorstein Eiriksson's companions were stricken by illness and many of them died there.

Thorstein asked that coffins be made for the bodies of those who had died, and that they be taken to the ship and secured away there – 'as when summer comes I intend to take all the bodies back to Eiriksfjord'.

It was not long until the sickness came to Thorstein's house, and his wife, Grimhild, was the first to fall ill. She was a very large woman, with the strength of a man, yet she bowed to the illness. Soon after that Thorstein Eiriksson was stricken, and both of them lay ill until Grimhild, the wife of Thorstein the Black, died.

After she had died, Thorstein the Black left the main room to seek a plank to place her body on.

Gudrid then spoke: 'Don't be away long, dear Thorstein,' she said.

He promised to do as she asked.

Thorstein Eiriksson then spoke: 'Strange are the actions of the mistress of the house now; she's struggling to raise herself up on her elbow, stretching her feet out from the bedboards and feeling for her shoes.'

At this Thorstein the Black returned and Grimhild collapsed that same instant, with a cracking sound coming from every timber in the room.

Thorstein then made a coffin for Grimhild's body and took it away and secured it. He was a large, strong man, and needed to call upon all his strength before he managed to remove his wife from the farm.

Thorstein Eiriksson's condition worsened and he died. His wife, Gudrid, was overtaken by grief. All of them were in the main room. Gudrid had been sitting on a stool in front of the bench where her husband, Thorstein, had lain.

Thorstein the farmer then took Gudrid from her stool into his arms and sat with her on the bench across from her husband Thorstein's corpse and said many encouraging things, consoling her and promising her that he would take her to Eiriksfjord with her husband Thorstein's body and those of his companions. 'And we'll invite other people to stay here,' he said, 'to provide you with solace and companionship.'

She thanked him.

Thorstein Eiriksson then sat up and spoke: 'Where is Gudrid?'

Three times he spoke these words, but she remained silent.

Then she spoke to Thorstein the farmer: 'Shall I answer his question or not?'

He told her not to answer. Thorstein the farmer then crossed the floor and sat on the chair and Gudrid on his knee.

Then Thorstein the farmer spoke: 'What is it you want, namesake?' he said.

He answered after a short pause: 'I want to tell Gudrid her fate, to make it easier for her to resign herself to my death, for I have gone to a good resting place. I can tell you, Gudrid, that you will be married to an Icelander, and you will live a long life together, and have many descendants, promising, bright and fine, sweet and well-scented. You will leave Greenland to go to Norway and from there to Iceland and set up house in Iceland. There you will live a long time, outliving your husband. You will travel abroad, go south on a pilgrimage and return to Iceland to your farm, where a church will be built. There you will remain and take holy orders and there you will die.'

At that Thorstein Eiriksson fell back, and his corpse was made ready and taken to the ship.

Thorstein the farmer kept all his promises to Gudrid faithfully. In the spring he sold his farm and livestock and loaded all his possessions aboard the ship with Gudrid. He made the ship ready and hired a crew and sailed to Eiriksfjord. The bodies were then buried in the churchyard.

Gudrid went to stay with Leif at Brattahlid, and Thorstein the Black built a farm in Eiriksfjord where he stayed as long as he lived, and was regarded as a most capable man.

6 | That same summer a ship from Norway arrived in Greenland. The skipper of the ship was named Thorfinn Karlsefni. He was the son of Thord Horse-head, the son of Snorri Thordarson of Hofdi.

Thorfinn Karlsefni was a very wealthy man. He spent the winter with Leif Eiriksson in Brattahlid. He was soon attracted by Gudrid and asked her to marry him, but she referred him to Leif for an answer. She was then engaged to him and their wedding took place that winter.

The discussion of a voyage to Vinland continued as before, and people strongly urged Karlsefni to make the journey, Gudrid among them. Once he had decided to make the journey he hired himself a crew of sixty men and five women.

Karlsefni and his crew made an agreement that anything of value they obtained would be divided equally among them. They took all sorts of livestock with them, for they intended to settle in the country if they could.

Karlsefni asked Leif for his houses in Vinland, and Leif said he would lend but not give them to him.

They then put out to sea in their ship and arrived without mishap at Leif's booths, where they unloaded their sleeping-sacks. They soon had plenty of good provisions, since a fine, large rorqual had stranded on the beach. After they had gone and carved up the whale they had no lack of food. The livestock made its way inland, but the male animals soon became irritable and hard to handle. They had brought one bull with them.

Karlsefni had trees felled and hewn to load aboard his ship and had the timber piled on a large rock to dry. They had plenty of supplies from the natural bounty there, including grapes, all sorts of fish and game, and other good things.

After the first winter passed and summer came, they became aware of natives. A large group of men came out of the woods close to where the cattle were pastured. The bull began bellowing and snorting very loudly. This frightened the natives, who ran off with their burdens, which included fur pelts and sables and all kinds of skins. They headed for Karlsefni's farm and tried to get into the house, but Karlsefni had the door defended. Neither group understood the language of the other.

The natives then set down their packs and opened them, offering their goods, preferably in exchange for weapons, but Karlsefni forbade the men to trade weapons.

He sought a solution by having the women bring out milk and milk products. Once they saw these products the natives wished to purchase them and nothing else. The trading with the natives resulted in them bearing off their purchases in their stomachs, leaving their packs and skins with Karlsefni and his companions. This done, they departed.

Karlsefni next had a sturdy palisade built around his farm, where they prepared to defend themselves. At this time Gudrid, Karlsefni's wife, gave birth to a boy, who was named Snorri. Near the beginning of their second winter the natives visited them again, in much greater numbers than before and with the same goods as before.

Karlsefni then spoke to the women: 'Bring out whatever food was most in demand last time, and nothing else.'

When the natives saw this they threw their packs in over the palisade. Gudrid sat inside in the doorway, with the cradle of her son, Snorri. A shadow fell across the doorway and a woman entered, rather short in stature, wearing a close-fitting tunic, with a shawl over her head and light red-brown hair. She was pale and had eyes so large that eyes of such size had never been seen in a human head.

She came to where Gudrid was sitting and spoke: 'What is your name?' she said.

'My name is Gudrid, and what is yours?'

'My name is Gudrid,' the other woman said.[15]

Gudrid, Karlsefni's wife, then motioned to her with her hand to sit down beside her, but just as she did so a great crash was heard and the woman disappeared. At that moment one of the natives had been killed by one of Karlsefni's servants for trying to take weapons from them, and they quickly ran off, leaving their clothes and trade goods lying behind. No one but Gudrid had seen the woman.

'We have to decide on a plan,' said Karlsefni, 'since I expect they will return for a third time, hostile and in greater numbers. We'll follow this plan: ten men will go out on this headland

and let themselves be seen there, while the rest of us go into the forest and cut a clearing for our cattle. When approaching from the forest we will take our bull and let him head our group into battle.'

In the place where they planned to take them on there was water on one side and a forest on the other. They followed the proposal Karlsefni had made.

The natives soon came to the place Karlsefni had intended for the battle. They fought and a large number of the natives were killed.

One of the men in the natives' group was tall and handsome, and Karlsefni thought him likely to be their leader.

One of the natives then picked up an axe, peered at it awhile and then aimed at one of his companions and struck him. The other fellow was killed outright. The tall man then picked up the axe, examined it awhile and then threw it as far out into the sea as he could. After that the natives fled into the woods at top speed, and they had no more dealings with them.

Karlsefni and his companions spent the entire winter there, but in the spring he declared that he wished to remain no longer and wanted to return to Greenland. They made ready for their journey, taking with them plenty of the land's products – grape-vines, berries and skins. They set sail and arrived safely in Eiriksfjord where they stayed over the winter.

7 | Discussion soon began again of a Vinland voyage, since the trip seemed to bring men both wealth and renown.

The same summer that Karlsefni returned from Vinland a ship arrived in Greenland from Norway. The skippers were two brothers, Helgi and Finnbogi, who spent the winter in Greenland. They were Icelanders, from the East Fjords.

We now turn to Freydis Eiriksdottir, who set out on a journey from Gardar to meet with the two brothers, Helgi and Finnbogi, and to propose that they all make the journey to Vinland on their ship and have a half-share of any profits from it. They agreed to this.

From there she went to her brother Leif and asked him to

give her the houses he had built in Vinland. He replied as he had before, that he would lend the houses but not give them to anyone.

According to the agreement between Freydis and the two brothers, each was to have thirty fighting men aboard his ship and women in addition. Freydis broke the agreement straight away, however, and took five extra men, concealing them so that the brothers were not aware of them until they had reached Vinland.

They put to sea, having agreed beforehand to try to stick together if possible on the way, and they almost managed this. The brothers arrived slightly earlier, however, and had un-loaded their ship and carried their belongings to Leif's houses when Freydis arrived. Her group unloaded their ship and carried its belongings up to the houses.

Freydis then said, 'Why did you put your belongings here?'

'We thought,' they answered, 'that you intended to keep your word to us.'

'Leif lent me the houses,' she said, 'not you.'

Helgi then spoke: 'We brothers will never be a match for your ill-will.' They removed their things and built themselves a longhouse farther from the sea, on the bank of a lake, and settled in well. Freydis had wood cut to make a load for her ship.

When winter came the brothers suggested that they hold games and arrange entertainment. This went on for a while, until disagreements arose. The ill-feelings split the party so that the games ceased and each group kept to its own houses. This continued for much of the winter.

Early one morning Freydis got up and dressed, but did not put on any footwear. The weather had left a thick dew on the grass. She took her husband's cape and placed it over her shoulders and went to the brothers' longhouse and came to the doorway. A man had gone out a short while earlier and left the door half-open. She opened the door and stood silently in the doorway awhile. Finnbogi lay awake at the inner end of the house.

He spoke: 'What do you want here, Freydis?'

She answered, 'I want you to get up and come outside. I have to speak to you.'

He did as she said. They went over to a tree trunk lying near the wall of the house and sat down there.

'How do you like it here?' she asked.

'I think the land has much to offer, but I don't like the ill-feeling between us, as I don't think there is reason for it.'

'What you say is true,' she said, 'and I agree. But my purpose in coming to see you was that I want to exchange ships with the two of you, as you have a larger ship than I do and I want to leave this place.'

'I suppose I can agree to that,' he said, 'if that will please you.'

After this they parted. She returned home and Finnbogi went back to his bed. When she climbed back into bed her cold feet woke Thorvard, who asked why she was so cold and wet.

She answered vehemently, 'I went to the brothers, to ask to purchase their ship, as I wanted a larger ship. They reacted so angrily; they struck me and treated me very badly, but you're such a coward that you will repay neither dishonour done to me nor to yourself. I am now paying the price of being so far from my home in Greenland, and unless you avenge this, I will divorce you!'[16]

Not being able to ignore her upbraiding any longer, he told the men to get up as quickly as they could and arm themselves. Having done so, they went at once to the longhouse of the brothers, entered while those inside were still asleep and took them, tied them up and, once bound, led them outside. Freydis, however, had each one of the men who was brought out killed.

Soon all the men had been killed and only the women were left, as no one would kill them.

Freydis then spoke: 'Hand me an axe.'

This was done, and she then attacked the five women there and killed them all.

They returned to their house after this wicked deed, and it was clear that Freydis was highly pleased with what she had accomplished. She spoke to her companions: 'If we are fortunate enough to make it back to Greenland,' she said, 'I will have anyone who tells of these events killed. We will say that they remained behind here when we took our leave.'

Early in the spring they loaded the ship, which the brothers had owned, with all the produce they could gather and the ship would hold. They then set sail and had a good voyage, sailing their ship into Eiriksfjord in early summer. Karlsefni was there already, with his ship all set to sail and only waiting for a favourable wind. It was said that no ship sailing from Greenland had been loaded with a more valuable cargo than the one he commanded.

8 | Freydis returned to her farm and livestock, which had not suffered from her absence. She made sure all her companions were well rewarded, since she wished to have her misdeeds concealed. She stayed on her farm after that.

Not everyone was so close-mouthed that they could keep silent about these misdeeds or wickedness, and eventually word got out. In time it reached the ears of Leif, her brother, who thought the story a terrible one.

Leif then took three men from Freydis's company and forced them all under torture to tell the truth about the events, and their accounts agreed in every detail.

'I am not the one to deal my sister, Freydis, the punishment she deserves,' Leif said, 'but I predict that their descendants will not get on well in this world.'

As things turned out, after that no one expected anything but evil from them.

To return to Karlsefni, he made his ship ready and set sail. They had a good passage and made land in Norway safely. He remained there over the winter, sold his goods, and both he and his wife were treated lavishly by the leading men in Norway. The following spring he made his ship ready to sail to Iceland.

When he was ready to sail and the ship lay at the landing stage awaiting a favourable wind, he was approached by a southerner, from Bremen in Saxony. He asked Karlsefni to sell him the carved decoration on the prow.[17]

'I don't care to sell it,' he replied.

'I'll give you half a mark of gold[18] for it,' the southerner said.

Karlsefni thought this a good offer and the purchase was concluded. The southerner then took the decoration and departed. Karlsefni did not know of what wood it was made, but it was of burl wood[19] which had been brought from Vinland.

Karlsefni then put to sea and made land in north Iceland, in Skagafjord, where he had his ship drawn ashore for the winter. In the spring he purchased the land at Glaumbaer and established his farm there, where he lived for the remainder of his days. He was the most respected of men. He and his wife, Gudrid, had a great number of descendants, and a fine clan they were.

After Karlsefni's death Gudrid took over the running of the household, together with her son Snorri who had been born in Vinland.

When Snorri married, Gudrid travelled abroad, made a pilgrimage south and returned to her son Snorri's farm. By then he had had a church built at Glaumbaer. Later Gudrid became a nun and anchoress,[20] staying there for the remainder of her life.

Snorri had a son named Thorgeir, who was the father of Yngveld, the mother of Bishop Brand. Snorri Karlsefnisson's daughter Hallfrid was the wife of Runolf, the father of Bishop Thorlak. Bjorn, another son of Karlsefni and Gudrid, was the father of Thorunn, the mother of Bishop Bjorn.[21]

There are a great number of people descended from Karlsefni, who founded a prosperous clan. It was Karlsefni who gave the most extensive reports of anyone of all of these voyages, some of which have now been set down in writing.

Translated by KENEVA KUNZ

EIRIK THE RED'S SAGA

1 | There was a warrior king named Oleif who was called
Oleif the White. He was the son of King Ingjald, who was
the son of Helgi, who was son of Olaf, who was son of Gudrod,
who was son of Halfdan White-leg, king of the people of
Oppland.[1]

Oleif went on Viking expeditions around Britain, conquering
the shire of Dublin, over which he declared himself king.[2] As
his wife he took Aud the Deep-minded, the daughter of Ketil
Flat-nose,[3] son of Bjorn Buna, an excellent man from Norway.
Their son was named Thorstein the Red.

After Oleif was killed in battle in Ireland, Aud and Thorstein
went to the Hebrides. There Thorstein married Thurid, the
daughter of Eyvind the Easterner and sister of Helgi the Lean.
They had a large number of children.

Thorstein became a warrior king, throwing in his lot with
Earl Sigurd the Powerful, the son of Eystein Glumra. They
conquered Caithness and Sutherland, Ross and Moray, and
more than half of Scotland. Thorstein became king there until
the Scots betrayed him and he was killed in battle.

Aud was at Caithness when she learned of the death of
Thorstein. She had a knorr built secretly in the forest and, when
it was finished, set out for the Orkneys. There she arranged the
marriage of Groa, Thorstein the Red's daughter. Groa was
the mother of Grelod, who was married to Earl Thorfinn the
Skull-splitter.[4]

After this Aud set out for Iceland. On her ship she had a crew
of twenty free-born men. Aud reached Iceland and spent the

first winter in Bjarnarhofn with her brother Bjorn. Afterwards Aud claimed all the land in the Dales between the Dagverdara and Skraumuhlaupsa rivers and settled at Hvamm. She used to pray on the Krossholar hill, where she had crosses erected, for she was baptized and a devout Christian. Accompanying her on her journey to Iceland were many men of good family who had been taken prisoner by Vikings raiding around Britain and were called bondsmen.

One of them was named Vifil. He was a man of very good family who had been taken prisoner in Britain[5] and was called a bondsman until Aud gave him his freedom. When Aud gave her crew farm sites, Vifil asked her why she had not given him one like the others. Aud replied that it made no difference [whether he owned land or not], he would be considered just as fine a man wherever he was. Aud gave him Vifilsdal and he settled there. He had a wife and two sons, Thorgeir and Thorbjorn. They were promising men and grew up with their father.

2 | There was a man named Thorvald, the son of Asvald Ulfsson, son of Ox-Thorir. His son was named Eirik the Red. Father and son left Jaeren and sailed to Iceland because [they had been involved in] slayings. They claimed land on the coast of Hornstrandir and settled at Drangar. There Thorvald died.

As his wife Eirik took Thjodhild, the daughter of Jorund Atlason.[6] Her mother, Thorbjorg Ship-breast, was married to Thorbjorn of Haukadal then. Eirik then moved south, cleared land in Haukadal and built a farm at Eiriksstadir by Vatnshorn.[7]

Eirik's slaves then caused a landslide to fall on the farm of Valthjof at Valthjofsstadir. His kinsman Filth-Eyjolf killed the slaves near Skeidsbrekkur above Vatnshorn. For this, Eirik slew Filth-Eyjolf. He also killed Hrafn the Dueller at Leikskalar. Geirstein and Odd of Jorvi, Eyjolf's kinsmen, sought redress for his killing.

After this Eirik was outlawed from Haukadal. He claimed the islands Brokey and Oxney and farmed at Tradir on Sudurey island the first winter. It was then Eirik lent Thorgest bedstead boards. Later he moved to Oxney where he farmed at Eiriks-stadir. He then asked for the bedstead boards back without success. Eirik went to Breidabolstad and took the boards, and Thorgest came after him. They fought not far from the farm at Drangar, where two of Thorgest's sons were killed, along with several other men.

After that both of them kept a large following. Eirik had the support of Styr and Eyjolf of Sviney, Thorbjorn Vifilsson and the sons of Thorbrand of Alftafjord, while Thord Bellower and Thorgeir of Hitardal, Aslak of Langadal and his son Illugi gave their support to Thorgest. Eirik and his companions were sentenced to outlawry at the Thorsnes Assembly. He made his ship ready in Eiriksvog and Eyjolf hid him in Dimunarvog while Thorgest and his men searched the islands for him. Thorbjorn, Eyjolf and Styr accompanied Eirik through the islands. Eirik said he intended to seek out the land that Gunnbjorn, the son of Ulf Crow, had seen when he was driven off course westward and discovered Gunnbjarnarsker (Gunnbjorn's skerry). If he found the land he promised to return to his friends and they parted with great warmth. Eirik promised to support them in any way he could if they should need his help.

Eirik sailed seaward from Snaefellsnes and approached land [in Greenland] under the glacier called Hvitserk (White shift). From there he sailed southwards, seeking suitable land for settlement.

He spent the first winter on Eiriksey island, near the middle of the eastern settlement. The following spring he travelled to Eiriksfjord where he settled. That summer he travelled around the [then] uninhabited western settlement, giving names to a number of sites. The second winter he spent in Eiriksholmar near Hvarfsgnipa, and the third summer he sailed as far north as Snaefell and into Hrafnsfjord. There he thought he had reached the head of Eiriksfjord. He then returned to spend the third winter in Eiriksey, at the mouth of Eiriksfjord.

The following summer he sailed to Iceland and made land in Breidafjord. He spent the winter with Ingolf at Holmlatur. The following spring he fought with Thorgest and lost, after which they made their peace.

In the summer Eirik left to settle in the country he had found, which he called Greenland, as he said people would be attracted there if it had a favourable name.

3 | Thorgeir Vifilsson took as his wife Arnora, the daughter of Einar of Laugarbrekka, the son of Sigmund, son of Ketil Thistle who had claimed land in Thistilfjord.

Einar had another daughter named Hallveig. She was married to Thorbjorn Vifilsson and was given land at Laugarbrekka, at Hellisvellir. Thorbjorn moved his household there and became a man of great worth. He ran a prosperous farm and lived in grand style. Gudrid was the name of Thorbjorn's daughter. She was the most attractive of women and one to be reckoned with in all her dealings.

A man named Orm farmed at Arnarstapi. His wife was named Halldis. Orm was a good farmer and a great friend of Thorbjorn's. The couple fostered Gudrid, who spent long periods of time there.

A man named Thorgeir farmed at Thorgeirsfell. He was very rich in livestock and was a freed slave. He had a son named Einar, a handsome and capable man, with a liking for fine dress. Einar went on trading voyages abroad, at which he was quite successful, and he usually spent the winters in Iceland and Norway by turn.

It is said that one autumn, when Einar was in Iceland, he travelled with his goods out to the Snaefellsnes peninsula, intending to sell them. He came to Arnarstapi and Orm invited him to stay with them, which Einar accepted, as friendship was included in the bargain. Einar's goods were placed in a shed. He took them out to show to Orm and his household, and asked Orm to choose as much as he wished for himself. Orm accepted and praised Einar as both a merchant of good repute and man of great fortune. While they were occupied with the goods a woman passed in front of the shed doorway.

Einar asked Orm who this beautiful woman was who had passed in front of the doorway – 'I haven't seen her here before.'

Orm said, 'That is Gudrid, my foster-daughter, the daughter of the farmer Thorbjorn of Laugarbrekka.'

Einar spoke: 'She'd make a fine match. Or has anyone already turned up to ask for her hand?'

Orm answered, 'She's been asked for right enough, my friend, but is no easy prize. As it turns out, she is choosy about her husband, as is her father as well.'

'Be that as it may,' Einar spoke, 'she's the woman I intend to propose to, and I would like you to put my proposal to her father, and if you do your best to support my suit I'll repay you with the truest of friendship. Farmer Thorbjorn should see that we'd be well connected, as he's a man of high repute and has a good farm, but I'm told his means have been much depleted. My father and I lack neither land nor means, so we'd be a considerable support to Thorbjorn if the match were concluded.'

Orm answered, 'Though I think of myself as your friend, I'm not eager to breach the question with him, for Thorbjorn is prone to take offence, and a man with no small sense of his own worth.'

Einar replied he would not be satisfied unless the proposal was made, and Orm said he would have his way. Einar headed south once more until he arrived back home.

Some time later Thorbjorn held an autumn feast, as was his custom, for he lived in high style. Orm from Arnarstapi attended and many other friends of Thorbjorn's.

Orm managed to speak privately to Thorbjorn and told him of the recent visit by Einar of Thorgeirsfell, who was becoming a man of promise. Orm then put Einar's proposal to Thorbjorn and said it would be suitable on a number of accounts – 'it would be a considerable support to you as far as money is concerned'.

Thorbjorn answered, 'I never expected to hear such words from you, telling me to marry my daughter to the son of a slave, as you suggest now, since you think I'm running short of money. She'll not go back with you, since you think her worthy of such a lowly match.'

Orm then returned home and all the other guests went to

their homes. Gudrid stayed behind with her father and spent that winter at home. When spring came Thorbjorn invited some friends to a feast. The provisions were plentiful, and it was attended by many people who enjoyed the finest of feasts.

During the feasting Thorbjorn called for silence, then spoke: 'Here I have lived a life of some length. I have enjoyed the kindness and warmth of others, and to my mind our dealings have gone well. My financial situation, however, which has not up to now been considered an unworthy one, is on the decline. So I would rather leave my farm than live with this loss of honour, and rather leave the country than shame my family. I intend to take up the offer made to me by my friend Eirik the Red, when he took his leave of me in Breidafjord. I intend to head for Greenland this summer if things go as I wish.'

These plans caused a great stir, as Thorbjorn had long been popular, but it was generally felt that once he had spoken in this way there would be little point in trying to dissuade him. Thorbjorn gave people gifts and the feast came to an end after this, with everyone returning to their homes.

Thorbjorn sold his lands and bought a ship which had been beached at the Hraunhafnaros estuary. Thirty men accompanied him on his voyage. Among them were Orm of Arnarstapi and his wife, and other friends of Thorbjorn's who did not want to part with him.

After this they set sail but the weather, which had been favourable when they set out, changed. The favourable wind dropped and they were beset by storms, so that they made little progress during the summer. Following this, illness plagued their company, and Orm and his wife and half the company died. The sea swelled and their boat took on much water but, despite many other hardships, they made land in Greenland at Herjolfsnes during the Winter Nights.

At Herjolfsnes lived a man named Thorkel. He was a capable man and the best of farmers. He gave Thorbjorn and all his companions shelter for the winter, treating them generously. Thorbjorn and all his companions were highly pleased.

4 | This was a very lean time in Greenland. Those who had gone hunting had had poor catches, and some of them had failed to return.

In the district there lived a woman named Thorbjorg, a seeress who was called the 'Little Prophetess'. She was one of ten sisters, all of whom had the gift of prophecy, and was the only one of them still alive.

It was Thorbjorg's custom to spend the winter visiting, one after another, farms to which she had been invited, mostly by people curious to learn of their own future or what was in store for the coming year. Since Thorkel was the leading farmer there, people felt it was up to him to try to find out when the hard times which had been oppressing them would let up. Thorkel invited the seeress to visit and preparations were made to entertain her well, as was the custom of the time when a woman of this type was received. A high seat was set for her, complete with cushion. This was to be stuffed with chicken feathers.

When she arrived one evening, along with the man who had been sent to fetch her, she was wearing a black mantle with a strap, which was adorned with precious stones right down to the hem. About her neck she wore a string of glass beads and on her head a hood of black lambskin lined with white catskin. She bore a staff with a knob at the top, adorned with brass set with stones on top. About her waist she had a linked charm belt with a large purse. In it she kept the charms which she needed for her predictions. She wore calfskin boots lined with fur, with long, sturdy laces and large pewter knobs on the ends. On her hands she wore gloves of catskin, white and lined with fur.

When she entered, everyone was supposed to offer her respectful greetings, and she responded according to how the person appealed to her. Farmer Thorkel took the wise woman by the hand and led her to the seat which had been prepared for her. He then asked her to survey his flock, servants and buildings. She had little to say about all of it.

That evening tables were set up and food prepared for the seeress. A porridge of kid's milk was made for her and as meat she was given the hearts of all the animals available there. She had a spoon of brass and a knife with an ivory shaft, its two halves clasped with bronze bands, and the point of which had broken off.

Once the tables had been cleared away, Thorkel approached Thorbjorg and asked what she thought of the house there and the conduct of the household, and how soon he could expect an answer to what he had asked and everyone wished to know. She answered that she would not reveal this until the next day after having spent the night there.

Late the following day she was provided with things she required to carry out her magic rites. She asked for women who knew the chants required for carrying out magic rites, which are called warlock songs.[8] But such women were not to be found. Then the people of the household were asked if there was anyone with such knowledge.

Gudrid answered, 'I have neither magical powers nor the gift of prophecy, but in Iceland my foster-mother, Halldis, taught me chants she called warlock songs.'

Thorbjorg answered, 'Then you know more than I expected.'

Gudrid said, 'These are the sort of actions in which I intend to take no part, because I am a Christian woman.'

Thorbjorg answered: 'It could be that you could help the people here by so doing, and you'd be no worse a woman for that. But I expect Thorkel to provide me with what I need.'

Thorkel then urged Gudrid, who said she would do as he wished. The women formed a warding ring around the platform raised for sorcery, with Thorbjorg perched atop it. Gudrid spoke the chant so well and so beautifully that people there said they had never heard anyone recite in a fairer voice.

The seeress thanked her for her chant. She said many spirits had been attracted who thought the chant fair to hear – 'though earlier they wished to turn their backs on us and refused to do our bidding. Many things are now clear to me which were earlier concealed from both me and others. And I can tell you that this spell of hardship will last no longer, and times will improve as the spring advances. The bout of illness which has long plagued you will also improve sooner than you expect. And you, Gudrid, I will reward on the spot for the help we have received, since your fate is now very clear to me. You will make the most honourable of matches here in Greenland, though you won't be putting down roots here, as your path leads to Iceland and from you will be descended a long and worthy line. Over all the branches of that family a bright ray will shine. May you fare well, now, my child.'

After that people approached the wise woman to learn what each of them was most curious to know. She made them good answer, and little that she predicted did not occur.

Following this an escort arrived from another farm and the seeress departed. Thorbjorn was also sent for, as he had refused to remain at home on the farm while such heathen practices were going on.

With the arrival of spring the weather soon improved, as Thorbjorg had predicted. Thorbjorn made his ship ready and sailed until he reached Brattahlid. Eirik received him with open arms and declared how good it was that he had come. Thorbjorn and his family spent the winter with him.

The following spring Eirik gave Thorbjorn land at Stokkanes, where he built an impressive farmhouse and lived from then on.

5 | Eirik had a wife named Thjodhild, and two sons, Thorstein and Leif.[9] Both of them were promising young men. Thorstein lived at home with his father, and there was no man in Greenland who was considered as handsome as he.

Leif had sailed to Norway where he was one of King Olaf Tryggvason's men.

But when Leif sailed from Greenland that summer the ship was driven off course to land in the Hebrides. From there they failed to get a favourable wind and had to stay in the islands for much of the summer.

Leif fell in love with a woman named Thorgunna. She was of very good family, and Leif realized that she knew a thing or two.

When Leif was leaving Thorgunna asked to go with him. Leif asked whether her kinsmen were of any mind to agree to this, and she declared she did not care. Leif said he was reluctant to

abduct a woman of such high birth from a foreign country –
'there are so few of us'.

Thorgunna spoke: 'I'm not sure you'll like the alternative
better.'

'I'll take my chances on that,' Leif said.

'Then I will tell you,' Thorgunna said, 'that I am with child,
and that this child is yours. It's my guess that I will give birth
to a boy, in due course. And even though you ignore him, I will
raise the boy and send him to you in Greenland as soon as
he is of an age to travel with others. But it's my guess that he
will serve you as well as you have served me now with your
departure. I intend to come to Greenland myself before it's all
over.'

He gave her a gold ring, a Greenland cape and a belt of
ivory.

The boy, who was named Thorgils, did come to Greenland
and Leif recognized him as his son. – Some men say that this
Thorgils came to Iceland before the hauntings at Froda[10] in the
summer. – Thorgils stayed in Greenland after that, and before
it was all over he was also thought to have something preter-
natural about him.

Leif and his men left the Hebrides and made land in Norway
in the autumn. Leif became one of the king's men, and King
Olaf Tryggvason showed him much honour, as Leif appeared
to him to be a man of good breeding.

On one occasion the king spoke to Leif privately and asked,
'Do you intend to sail to Greenland this summer?'

Leif answered, 'I would like to do so, if it is your wish.'

The king answered, 'It could well be so; you will go as my
envoy and convert Greenland to Christianity.'

Leif said the king should decide that, but added that he feared
this message would meet with a harsh reception in Greenland.
The king said he saw no man more suitable for the job than
Leif – 'and you'll have the good fortune that's needed'.

'If that's so,' Leif declared, 'then only because I enjoy yours
as well.'

Once he had made ready, Leif set sail. After being tossed
about at sea for a long time he chanced upon land where he

had not expected any to be found. Fields of self-sown wheat[11] and vines were growing there; also, there were trees known as burl,[12] and they took specimens of all of them.

Leif also chanced upon men clinging to a ship's wreck, whom he brought home and found shelter for over the winter. In so doing he showed his strong character and kindness. He converted the country to Christianity.[13] Afterwards he became known as Leif the Lucky.

Leif made land in Eiriksfjord and went home to the farm at Brattahlid. There he was received warmly. He soon began to advocate Christianity and the true catholic faith throughout the country, revealing the messages of King Olaf Tryggvason to the people, and telling them how excellent and glorious this faith was.

Eirik was reluctant to give up his faith, but Thjodhild was quick to convert and had a church built a fair distance from the house. It was called Thjodhild's church[14] and there she prayed, along with those other people who converted to Christianity, of whom there were many. After her conversion, Thjodhild refused to sleep with Eirik, much to his displeasure.

The suggestion that men go to seek out the land which Leif had found soon gained wide support. The leading proponent was Eirik's son, Thorstein, a good, wise and popular man. Eirik was also urged to go, as people valued most his good fortune and leadership. For a long time he was against going, but when his friends urged him he did not refuse.

They made ready the ship on which Thorbjorn had sailed to Greenland, with twenty men to go on the journey. They took few trading goods, but all the more weapons and provisions.

The morning that he left, Eirik took a small chest containing gold and silver. He hid the money and then went on his way. After going only a short way he fell from his horse, breaking several ribs and injuring his shoulder, so that he cried out, 'Ow, ow!' Because of his mishap he sent word to his wife to retrieve the money he had hidden, saying he had been punished for having hidden it.

They then sailed out of Eiriksfjord in fine spirits, pleased with their prospects.

They were tossed about at sea for a long time and failed to reach their intended destination. They came in sight of Iceland and noticed birds from Ireland. Their ship was driven to and fro across the sea until they returned to Greenland in the autumn, worn out and in poor shape, and made land when it was almost winter in Eiriksfjord.

Eirik then spoke: 'More cheerful we were in the summer to leave this fjord than now to return to it, though we have much to welcome us.'

Thorstein spoke: 'We'd be doing the generous thing by seeing to those men who have no house to go to and providing for them over the winter.'

Eirik answered, 'It's usually true, as they say, that you can't know a good question until you have the answer, and so it'll turn out here. We'll do as you say.'

All those men who had no other house to go to were taken in by father and son for the winter. They went home to Brattahlid then and spent the winter there.

6 | The next thing to be told of is the proposal made by Thorstein Eiriksson to Gudrid Thorbjarnardottir. He was given a favourable answer by both Gudrid and her father, and so Thorstein married Gudrid and their wedding was held at Brattahlid that autumn. The wedding feast was a grand one and the guests were many.

Thorstein had a farm and livestock in the western settlement at a place called Lysufjord. A man there named Thorstein owned a half-share in this farm; his wife was named Sigrid. Thorstein and Gudrid went to his namesake in Lysufjord that autumn where they were received warmly. They spent the winter there.

It then happened that sickness struck the farm shortly after the beginning of winter. The foreman, named Gardi, was an unpopular man. He was the first to fall ill and die. It was not long until the inhabitants caught the sickness, one after the other and died, until Thorstein Eiriksson and Sigrid, the farmer's wife, fell ill, too.

One evening Sigrid wanted to go to the outhouse which stood opposite the door of the farmhouse. Gudrid went with her and as they looked at the doorway Sigrid cried, 'Oh!'

Gudrid spoke: 'We have acted carelessly, you shouldn't be exposed to the cold at all; we must get back inside as quickly as we can!'

Sigrid answered, 'I won't go out with things as they are! All of those who are dead are standing there before the door; among them I recognize your husband Thorstein and myself as well. How horrible to see it!'

When it had passed, she spoke: 'I don't see them now.'

Thorstein, whom she had seen with a whip in his hand, ready to strike the dead, had also disappeared. They then entered the house.

Before morning came she was dead and a coffin was made for her body. That same day men were going fishing and Thorstein accompanied them down to where the boats were beached. Towards dusk he went again to check on their catch. Then Thorstein Eiriksson sent him word to come to him, saying there was no peace at home as the farmer's wife was trying to rise up and get into the bed with him. When he entered she had reached the sideboards of the bed. He took hold of her and drove an axe into her breast.

Thorstein Eiriksson died near sundown. Thorstein told Gudrid to lie down and sleep; he would keep watch over the bodies that night, he said. Gudrid did so and soon fell asleep.

Only a little of the night had passed when Thorstein rose up, saying that he wished Gudrid to be summoned and wanted to speak to her: 'It is God's will that I be granted an exception for this brief time to improve my prospects.'

Thorstein went to Gudrid, woke her and told her to cross herself and ask the Lord for help – 'Thorstein Eiriksson has spoken to me and said he wanted to see you. It is your decision; I will not advise you either way.'

She answered, 'It may be that there is a purpose for this strange occurrence, and it will have consequences long to be remembered. I expect that God will grant me his protection. I will take the chance, with God's mercy, of speaking to him, as I cannot escape any threat to myself. I would rather he need not look farther, and I suspect that would be the alternative.'

Gudrid then went to see Thorstein, and he seemed to her to shed tears. He spoke several words in her ear in a low voice, so that she alone heard, and said that those men rejoiced who kept their faith well and it brought mercy and salvation. Yet he said many kept their faith poorly.

'These practices will not do which have been followed here in Greenland after the coming of Christianity: burying people in unconsecrated ground with little if any service said over them. I want to have my corpse taken to a church, along with those of the other people who have died here. But Gardi should be burned on a pyre straight away, as he has caused all the hauntings which have occurred here this winter.'

He also spoke of his situation and declared that her future held great things in store, but he warned her against marrying a Greenlander. He also asked her to donate their money to a church or to poor people, and then he sank down for the second time.

It had been common practice in Greenland, since Christianity had been adopted, to bury people in unconsecrated ground on the farms where they died. A pole was set up on the breast of each corpse until a priest came, then the pole was pulled out and consecrated water poured into the hole and a burial service performed, even though this was only done much later.

The bodies were taken to the church in Eiriksfjord, and priests held burial services for them.

After this Thorbjorn died. All of his money went to Gudrid. Eirik invited her to live with them and saw that she was well provided for.

7 | There was a man named Thorfinn Karlsefni, the son of Thord Horse-head who lived in north Iceland, at the place now called Reynines in Skagafjord. Karlsefni was a man of good family and good means.[15] His mother was named Thorunn. He went on trading voyages and was a merchant of good repute.

One summer Karlsefni made his ship ready for a voyage to Greenland. Snorri Thorbrandsson[16] of Alftafjord was to accompany him and they took a party of forty men with them.

A man named Bjarni Grimolfsson, from Breidafjord, and another named Thorhall Gamlason,[17] from the East Fjords, made their ship ready the same summer as Karlsefni and were also heading for Greenland. There were forty men on their ship. The two ships set sail once they had made ready.

There is no mention of how long they were at sea. But it is said that both these ships sailed into Eiriksfjord that autumn.

Eirik rode to the ships, along with other Greenlanders, and busy trading commenced. The skippers of the vessels invited Eirik to take his pick of their wares, and Eirik repaid them generously, as he invited both crews home to stay the winter with him in Brattahlid. This the merchants accepted and went home with him. Their goods were later transported to Brattahlid, where there was no lack of good and ample outbuildings to store them in. The merchants were highly pleased with their winter stay with Eirik.

But as Yule approached, Eirik grew sadder than was his wont. On one occasion Karlsefni spoke to him privately and asked, 'Is something troubling you, Eirik? You seem to me to be more silent than before. You have treated us very generously, and we owe it to you to repay you by any means we can. Tell me what is causing your sadness.'

Eirik answered, 'You have also accepted with gratitude and respect, and I don't feel that your contribution to our exchange has been lacking in any way. But I'll regret it if word gets round that you've spent here a Yuletide as lean as the one now approaching.'

Karlsefni answered, 'It won't be that at all. We've malt and flour and grain aboard our ships, and you may help yourself to them as you will, to prepare a feast worthy of your generous hospitality.'

Eirik accepted this. Preparations for a Yule feast began, which proved to be so bountiful that men could scarcely recall having seen its like.

After Yule Karlsefni approached Eirik to ask for Gudrid's hand, as it seemed to him that she was under Eirik's protection, and both an attractive and knowledgeable woman. Eirik answered that he would support his suit, and that she was a fine match – 'and it's likely that her fate will turn out as prophesied,' he added, even if she did marry Karlsefni, whom he knew to be a worthy man. The subject was broached with Gudrid and she allowed herself to be guided by Eirik's advice. No more needs to be said on that point, except that the match was agreed and the celebrations extended to include the wedding which took place.

That winter there was much merrymaking in Brattahlid; many board games were played, there was storytelling and plenty of other entertainment to brighten the life of the household.

8 | There were great discussions that winter in Brattahlid of Snorri and Karlsefni setting sail for Vinland,[18] and people talked at length about it. In the end Snorri and Karlsefni made their vessel ready, intending to sail in search of Vinland that summer. Bjarni and Thorhall decided to accompany them on the voyage, taking their own ship and their companions who had sailed with them on the voyage out.

A man named Thorvard was married to Freydis, who was an illegitimate daughter of Eirik the Red. He went with them, along with Thorvald, Eirik's son, and Thorhall who was called the Huntsman. For years he had accompanied Eirik on hunting trips in the summers, and was entrusted with many tasks. Thorhall was a large man, dark and coarse-featured; he was getting on in years and difficult to handle. He was a silent man, who was not generally given to conversation, devious and yet insulting in his speech, and who usually did his best to make trouble. He had paid scant heed to the faith since it had come to Greenland. Thorhall was not popular with most people but he had long been in Eirik's confidence. He was among those on the ship with Thorvald and Thorvard, as he had a wide knowledge of the uninhabited regions.[19] They had the ship which Thorbjorn had brought to Greenland and set sail with Karlsefni and his group. Most of the men aboard were from Greenland. The crews of the three ships made a hundred plus forty men.

They sailed along the coast to the western settlement, then to the Bear islands[20] and from there with a northerly wind. After two days at sea they sighted land and rowed over in boats to explore it. There they found many flat slabs of stone, so large that two men could lie foot-to-foot across them. There were many foxes there. They gave the land the name Helluland (Stone-slab land).[21]

After that they sailed with a northerly wind for two days, and again sighted land, with large forests and many animals. An island lay to the south-east, off the coast, where they discovered a bear, and they called it Bjarney (Bear Island), and the forested land itself Markland.[22]

After another two days passed they again sighted land and approached the shore where a peninsula jutted out. They sailed upwind along the coast, keeping the land on the starboard. The country was wild with a long shoreline and sand flats. They rowed ashore in boats and, discovering the keel of a ship there,[23] named this point Kjalarnes (Keel point). They also gave the beaches the name Furdustrandir (Wonder beaches) for their surprising length. After this the coastline was indented with numerous inlets which they skirted in their ships.

When Leif had served King Olaf Tryggvason and was told by him to convert Greenland to Christianity, the king had given him two Scots, a man named Haki and a woman called Hekja. The king told him to call upon them whenever he needed someone with speed, as they were fleeter of foot than any deer. Leif and Eirik had sent them to accompany Karlsefni.

After sailing the length of the Furdustrandir, they put the two Scots ashore and told them to run southwards to explore the country and return before three days' time had elapsed. They were dressed in a garment known as a *kjafal*,[24] which had a hood at the top but no arms, and was open at the sides and fastened between the legs with a button and loop; they wore nothing else.

The ships cast anchor and lay to during this time.

After three days had passed the two returned to the shore, one of them with grapes in hand and the other with self-sown wheat. Karlsefni said that they had found good land. After taking them on board once more, they sailed onwards, until they reached a fjord cutting into the coast. They steered the ships into the fjord with an island near its mouth, where there were strong currents, and called the island Straumsey (Stream island). There were so many birds there that they could hardly walk without stepping on eggs. They sailed up into the fjord, which they called Straumsfjord, unloaded the cargo from the ships and began settling in.

They had brought all sorts of livestock with them and explored the land and its resources. There were mountains there, and a pleasant landscape. They paid little attention to things other than exploring the land. The grass there grew tall.

They spent the winter there, and it was a harsh winter, for which they had made little preparation, and they grew short of food and caught nothing when hunting or fishing. They went out to the island, expecting to find some prey to hunt or food on the beaches. They found little food, but their livestock improved there. After this they entreated God to send them something to eat, but the response was not as quick in coming as their need was urgent. Thorhall disappeared and men went to look for him. They searched for three days, and on the fourth Karlsefni and Bjarni found him at the edge of a cliff. He was staring skywards, with his mouth, nostrils and eyes wide open, scratching and pinching himself and mumbling something.

They asked what he was doing there, and he replied that it made no difference. He said they need not look so surprised and said for most of his life he had got along without their advice. They told him to come back with them and he did so.

Shortly afterwards they found a beached whale and flocked to the site to carve it up, although they failed to recognize what type it was. Karlsefni had a wide knowledge of whales, but even he did not recognize it. The cooks boiled the meat and they ate it, but it made everyone ill.

Thorhall then came up and spoke: 'Didn't Old Redbeard[25] prove to be more help than your Christ? This was my payment for the poem I composed about Thor, my guardian, who's seldom disappointed me.'

Once they heard this no one wanted to eat the whale meat, they cast it off a cliff and threw themselves on God's mercy. The weather improved so they could go fishing, and from then on they had supplies in plenty.

In the spring they moved further into Straumsfjord and lived on the produce of both shores of the fjord: hunting game inland, gathering eggs on the island and fishing at sea.

9 | They then began to discuss and plan the continuation of their journey. Thorhall wanted to head north, past Furdustrandir and around Kjalarnes to seek Vinland.[26] Karlsefni wished to sail south along the east shore, feeling the land would be more substantial the farther south it was, and he felt it was advisable to explore both.

Thorhall then made his ship ready close to the island, with no more than nine men to accompany him. The rest of their company went with Karlsefni.

One day as Thorhall was carrying water aboard his ship he drank of it and spoke this verse:

1. With promises of fine drinks
   the war-trees wheedled,   *war-trees: warriors*
   spurring me to journey
   to these scanty shores.
   War-oak of the helmet god,   *war-oak: warrior, helmet god: Odin*
   I now wield but a bucket,
   no sweet wine do I sup
   stooping at the spring.

After that they set out, and Karlsefni followed them as far as the island. Before hoisting the sail Thorhall spoke this verse:

2. We'll return to where
   our countrymen await us,
   head our sand-heaven's horse   *sand-heaven:* sea, its *horse:* ship
   to scout the ship's wide plains.   *ship's . . . plains:* seas
   Let the wielders of sword storms   *wielders of sword storms:* warriors
   laud the land, unwearied,
   settle Wonder Beaches
   and serve up their whale.

They then separated and Thorhall and his crew sailed north
past Furdustrandir and Kjalarnes, and from there attempted to
sail to the west of it. But they ran into storms and were driven
ashore in Ireland, where they were beaten and enslaved. There
Thorhall died.

10 | Karlsefni headed south around the coast, with Snorri and
     | Bjarni and the rest of their company. They sailed a long
time, until they came to a river which flowed into a lake and
from there into the sea. There were wide sandbars beyond the
mouth of the river, and they could only sail into the river at
high tide. Karlsefni and his company sailed into the lagoon and
called the land Hop (Tidal pool). There they found fields of
self-sown wheat in the low-lying areas and vines growing on
the hills. Every stream was teeming with fish. They dug trenches
along the high-water mark and when the tide ebbed there were
flounder[27] in them. There were a great number of deer of all
kinds in the forest.

They stayed there for a fortnight, enjoying themselves and
finding nothing unusual. They had taken their livestock with
them.

Early one morning they noticed nine hide-covered boats, and
the people in them waved wooden poles that made a swishing
sound as they turned them around sunwise.

Karlsefni then spoke: 'What can this mean?'

Snorri replied: 'It may be a sign of peace; we should take a
white shield and lift it up in return.'

This they did.

The others then rowed towards them and were astonished at the sight of them as they landed on the shore. They were short in height with threatening features and tangled hair on their heads. Their eyes were large and their cheeks broad. They stayed there awhile, marvelling, then rowed away again to the south around the point.

The group had built their booths up above the lake, with some of the huts farther inland, and others close to the shore.

They remained there that winter. There was no snow at all and the livestock could fend for themselves out of doors.

11 | One morning, as spring advanced, they noticed a large number of hide-covered boats rowing up from the south around the point. There were so many of them that it looked as if bits of coal had been tossed over the water, and there was a pole waving from each boat. They signalled with their shields and began trading with the visitors, who mostly wished to trade for red cloth. They also wanted to purchase swords and spears, but Karlsefni and Snorri forbade this. They traded dark pelts for the cloth, and for each pelt they took cloth a hand in length, which they bound about their heads.

This went on for some time, until there was little cloth left. They then cut the cloth into smaller pieces, each no wider than a finger's width, but the natives gave just as much for it or more.

At this point a bull, owned by Karlsefni and his companions, ran out of the forest and bellowed loudly. The natives took fright at this, ran to their boats and rowed off to the south. Three weeks passed and there was no sign of them.

After that they saw a large group of native boats approach from the south, as thick as a steady stream. They were waving poles counter-sunwise now and all of them were shrieking loudly. The men took up their red shields and went towards them. They met and began fighting. A hard barrage rained down and the natives also had catapults. Karlsefni and Snorri then saw the natives lift up on poles a large round object,[28] about the size of a sheep's gut and black in colour, which came

flying up on the land and made a threatening noise when it
landed. It struck great fear into Karlsefni and his men, who
decided their best course was to flee upriver, since the native
party seemed to be attacking from all sides, until they reached
a cliff wall where they could put up a good fight.

Freydis came out of the camp as they were fleeing. She called,
'Why do you flee such miserable opponents, men like you who
look to me to be capable of killing them off like sheep? Had I
a weapon I'm sure I would fight better than any of you.' They
paid no attention to what she said. Freydis wanted to go with
them, but moved somewhat slowly, as she was with child. She
followed them into the forest, but the natives reached her. She
came across a slain man, Thorbrand Snorrason, who had been
struck in the head by a slab of stone. His sword lay beside him,
and this she snatched up and prepared to defend herself with it
as the natives approached her. Freeing one of her breasts from
her shift, she smacked the sword with it. This frightened the
natives, who turned and ran back to their boats and rowed
away.

Karlsefni and his men came back to her and praised her
luck.

Two of Karlsefni's men were killed and many of the natives
were slain, yet Karlsefni and his men were outnumbered. They
returned to the booths wondering who these numerous people
were who had attacked them on land. But it now looked to
them as if the company in the boats had been the sole attackers,
and any other attackers had only been an illusion.

The natives also found one of the dead men, whose axe lay
beside him. One of them picked up the axe and chopped at a
tree, and then each took his turn at it. They thought this thing
which cut so well a real treasure. One of them struck a stone
and the axe broke. He thought a thing which could not withstand stone to be of little worth, and tossed it away.

The party then realized that, despite everything the land had
to offer there, they would be under constant threat of attack
from its prior inhabitants. They made ready to depart for their
own country. Sailing north along the shore, they discovered

five natives sleeping in skin sacks near the shore. Beside them they had vessels filled with deer marrow blended with blood.[29] They assumed these men to be outlaws and killed them.

They then came to a headland thick with deer. The point looked like a huge dunghill, as the deer gathered there at night to sleep. They then entered Straumsfjord, where they found food in plenty. Some people say that Bjarni and Gudrid had remained behind there with a hundred others and gone no farther, and that it was Karlsefni and Snorri who went further south with some forty men, stayed no more than two months at Hop and returned the same summer.

The group stayed there while Karlsefni went on one ship to look for Thorhall. They sailed north around Kjalarnes and then westwards of it, keeping the land on their port side. They saw nothing but wild forest. When they had sailed for a long time they reached a river flowing from east to west. They sailed into the mouth of the river and lay to near the south bank.

12 | One morning Karlsefni's men saw something shiny above a clearing in the trees, and they called out. It moved and proved to be a one-legged creature[30] which darted down to where the ship lay tied. Thorvald, Eirik the Red's son, was at the helm, and the one-legged man shot an arrow into his intestine. Thorvald drew the arrow out and spoke: 'Fat paunch that was. We've found a land of fine resources, though we'll hardly enjoy much of them.' Thorvald died from the wound shortly after. The one-legged man then ran off back north. They pursued him and caught glimpses of him now and again. He then fled into a cove and they turned back.

One of the men then spoke this verse:

3. True it was
   that our men tracked
   a one-legged creature
   down to the shore.
   The uncanny fellow

fled in a flash,
though rough was his way,
hear us, Karlsefni!

They soon left to head northwards where they thought they sighted the Land of the One-Legged, but did not want to put their lives in further danger. They saw mountains which they felt to be the same as those near Hop, and both these places seemed to be equally far away from Straumsfjord.

They returned to spend their third winter in Straumsfjord. Many quarrels arose, as the men who had no wives sought to take those of the married men. Karlsefni's son Snorri was born there the first autumn and was three years old when they left.

They had southerly winds and reached Markland, where they met five natives. One was bearded, two were women and two of them children. Karlsefni and his men caught the boys but the others escaped and disappeared into the earth. They took the boys with them and taught them their language and had them baptized. They called their mother Vethild and their father Ovaegi. They said that kings ruled the land of the natives; one of them was called Avaldamon and the other Valdidida.[31] No houses were there, they said, but people slept in caves or holes. They spoke of another land, across from their own. There people dressed in white clothing, shouted loudly and bore poles and waved banners. This people assumed to be the land of the white men.[32]

They then came to Greenland and spent the winter with Eirik the Red.

13 | Bjarni Grimolfsson and his group were borne into the Greenland Straits and entered Madkasjo (Sea of Worms), although they failed to realize it until the ship under them had become infested with shipworms. They then discussed what to do. They had a ship's boat in tow which had been smeared with tar made of seal blubber. It is said that shell maggots cannot infest wood smeared with such tar. The majority proposed to set as many men into the boat as it could carry. When this

was tried, it turned out to have room for no more than half of them.

Bjarni then said they should decide by lot who should go in the boat, and not decide by status. Although all of the people there wanted to go into the boat, it couldn't take them all. So they decided to draw lots to decide who would board the boat and who would remain aboard the trading vessel. The outcome was that it fell to Bjarni and almost half of those on board to go in the boat.

Those who had been selected left the ship and boarded the boat.

Once they were aboard the boat one young Icelander, who had sailed with Bjarni, called out to him, 'Are you going to desert me now, Bjarni?'

'So it must be,' Bjarni answered.

He said, 'That's not what you promised me when I left my father's house in Iceland to follow you.'

Bjarni answered, 'I don't see we've much other choice now. What would you advise?'

He said, 'I see the solution – that we change places, you come up here and I'll take your place there.'

'So be it,' Bjarni answered, 'as I see you put a high price on life and are very upset about dying.'

They then changed places. The man climbed into the boat and Bjarni aboard the ship. People say that Bjarni died there in the Sea of Worms, along with the others on board his ship. The ship's boat and those on it went on their way and made land, after which they told this tale.[33]

14 | The following summer Karlsefni sailed for Iceland and Gudrid with him. He came home to his farm at Reynines.

His mother thought his match hardly worthy, and Gudrid did not stay on the farm the first winter. But when she learned what an outstanding woman Gudrid was, Gudrid moved to the farm and the two women got along well.

Karlsefni's son Snorri had a daughter, Hallfrid, who was the mother of Bishop Thorlak Runolfsson.

Karlsefni and Gudrid had a son named Thorbjorn, whose daughter Thorunn was the mother of Bishop Bjorn.

Thorgeir, son of Snorri Karlsefni, was the father of Yngveld, the mother of the first Bishop Brand.[34]

And here ends this saga.[35]

Translated by KENEVA KUNZ

Notes

THE SAGA OF THE GREENLANDERS

1. *Ingolf, the settler of Iceland*: Ingolf Arnarson was the first settler
    in Iceland in 874 and built his farm in Reykjavík, on the site of
    what is now the capital. He is said to have claimed the entire
    peninsula of Reykjanes and the surrounding territory in the
    south-west, and to have given large portions of it to friends and
    family who arrived later.

2. *the drapa of the Sea Fences (Breakers)*: For 'drapa', see Glossary.
    The *Hauksbók* version of *The Book of Settlements*, written by
    lawspeaker Hauk Erlendsson in the early 1300s, also refers to
    this poem and cites two additional lines. It is believed that the
    poem is linked with the story in *The Book of Settlements* about
    twenty-five ships accompanying Eirik the Red when he left Ice-
    land to settle in Greenland in 985 or 986 – but only fourteen
    ships survived the crossing because of the rough seas. There has
    been speculation about an underwater earthquake causing this
    great loss, so the 'sea fences' (i.e. breakers) refer to a tsunami
    effect. For Eirik's early years, see Chapter 2 of *Eirik the Red's
    Saga*.

3. *before sighting land . . . nothing of use*: Since we do not know if
    'days' refers to 12 or 24 hours (the Icelandic *dœgur* could mean
    either), we can't calculate the voyage; the saga wasn't intended
    as a logbook. The passage should be read as an introduction for
    orientation in the new world that is about to be described in
    greater detail. Thus the audience can now visualize three lands
    from south to north; the first two are forested but the northern-
    most has only mountains and a glacier (see Maps on pp. 63–64).
    This is a reasonable first description of the lands west and south
    from Greenland: Newfoundland, Labrador and Baffin Island.

4. *Earl Eirik*: Ruled in Norway, 1000–1012, which makes it problematic how Bjarni is supposed to have been received by him shortly after his voyage to Greenland in the wake of Eirik the Red's settlement there in 985 or 986. It has been suggested that the scribe of *Flateyjarbók* misread an abbreviated form 'Er' (Eirik the Red) as 'Ej' ('Eirik *jarl* = earl') and was then obliged to send Bjarni away from Greenland before he started telling stories about his discovery ('r' and 'j' would look very similar in manuscript). In the context it makes much better sense that Bjarni, after meeting up with his family, should have gone to the leader of the new settlement in Greenland, Eirik the Red, to report the new lands he had discovered, thus instigating 'much talk of looking for new lands'. The fact that the scribe of *Flateyjarbók* wrote the saga into a compilation where a long episode from the *Saga of King Olaf Tryggvason* is inserted between Chapters 1 and 2 of *The Saga of the Greenlanders* could explain this discrepancy.

5. *Tyrkir, from a more southerly country*: The role of Tyrkir, his southerly origins and his German language serve to authenticate his identification of the grapevines and grapes.

6. *Markland (Forest land)*: The first two lands named by Leif must be taken to be the last two lands sighted by Bjarni: probably Baffin Island and Labrador.

7. *with a north-easterly wind before they saw land*: Even though Viking Age ships could sail in almost any direction, this is a traditional saga device for describing the direction in which ships are supposed to have sailed. The audience would visualize Leif's ship sailing south-west from the second land sighted by Bjarni and crossing open water for two days before coming to the idyllic island north of the mainland, and separated from it by a sound and extensive shallows. (It doesn't make sense to have Leif exploring the eastern coast of Newfoundland, whereas sending him into the Gulf of St Lawrence solves the problem.)

8. *this salmon was larger than they had ever seen before*: According to the marine biologist David Cairns of the University of Prince Edward Island in Charlottetown and the Canadian Department of Fisheries and Oceans, salmon enter the rivers of Prince Edward Island, northern Nova Scotia and south-eastern New Brunswick for breeding after two or more years at sea (that is, *two-* or *multi-sea-winter salmon*), as opposed to just one year in Newfoundland (known as *grilse*, which dominate the rivers in Newfoundland).

9. *mid-morning and still visible at mid-afternoon*: This passage has

been interpreted in conflicting ways, and the latitude has been calculated as between 31°N and 50°N. Apart from the fact that the text refers to 'the depth of winter' rather than using the more precise 'solstice', there is a problem in precisely how the words translated as 'mid-morning' and 'mid-afternoon' should be interpreted. Their general sense is where the sun is at around 9 a.m. and 3–3:30 p.m., respectively, but the question arises as to whether the reference is to time or to the position on the horizon where the sun sets and rises. Gustav Storm (1886), with the help of the astronomer Hans Geelmuyden, made a thorough and determined attempt to solve this problem late in the nineteenth century and concluded that Leif's reading had been made a little to the south of about 50°N, the latitude of northern Newfoundland; this was reckoned to be too far north at the time, when the dominant view was that Vinland lay somewhere in New England, and Storm's work was largely ignored. Recently the matter has been taken up again by Páll Bergþórsson, *The Wineland Millennium: Saga and Evidence* (Reykjavík, 2000), pp. 161–5, who deduces that the reference is to the direction and position of the sun on the horizon at sunrise and sunset, and this corresponds fairly accurately to the latitude of L'Anse aux Meadows. Apart from this observation, it is impossible to make Leif's voyage incorporate L'Anse aux Meadows (except for the frostless winters in good years), but it fits the southern shores of the Gulf of St Lawrence, around Prince Edward Island and the Miramichi Bay in New Brunswick (see Introduction, pp. xxxiv–xxxv). It is quite possible that the saga does not differentiate between the explorations in the southerly regions and the winter camp.

10. *grapevines and grapes*: See Introduction, p. xxix.

11. *and called it Vinland (Wineland)*: See Introduction, p. xxix.

12. *going north around the land*: The directions, first to the west of the land and then on the eastern side where Thorvald's camp is located, make sense if the camp is located just west of the northernmost tip of Newfoundland, i.e. in L'Anse aux Meadows.

13. *Kjalarnes (Keel point)*: The place name also appears in Chapter 8 of *Eirik the Red's Saga*, in the account of Karlsefni and Gudrid's voyage, which may be assumed to indicate an awareness of the Keel point mentioned here, enabling the audience/readers to build up a mental map of the entire area (see Introduction, pp. xxx–xxxiii). The episode is a general warning to seafarers to avoid sailing south on the eastern side of the land; rather they should go south and west, along the western shore.

14. *natives*: The word in early Icelandic sources for the native people of Greenland and North America, 'Skraelings', does not differentiate between Inuit and Indians.

15. *'My name is Gudrid,' the other woman said*: In order to explain the native woman's peculiar answer, the folklorist Bo Almqvist has pointed to many instances, from North America in particular, where Europeans meet natives for the first time who repeat their own words without knowing the meaning ('"My Name is Guðríðr": An Enigmatic Episode in *Grænlendinga saga*', in *Approaches to Vinland*, ed. Andrew Wawn and Þórunn Sigurðardóttir (Reykjavík, 2001), pp. 15–30).

16. *I will divorce you*: According to the Icelandic legal codex *Grágás*, from the commonwealth period, women had the same right as men to declare divorce, and they could also claim their share of the estate – if they had valid grounds for their declaration.

17. *the carved decoration on the prow*: The Icelandic *húsasnotra* could refer not to a decoration but to a kind of astrolabe.

18. *half a mark of gold*: Such a high price that the audience is clearly meant to think of the *húsasnotra* from Vinland as exceptionally valuable – possibly because of its exotic origins. It is noteworthy that the southerner who buys it is said to come from Bremen in Saxony (it is from the writings of Adam of Bremen that we hear first of Vinland, in his work from around 1075; see Introduction, p. xxxviii).

19. *burl wood*: There is ample evidence that this is the meaning of the word *mösur*. Burls are still used for woodcarving and decorative objects. See also Introduction, p. xxxvii, and *Eirik the Red's Saga* note 12.

20. *Gudrid became a nun and anchoress*: A convent was only established at Reynines in Skagafjord (where Karlsefni and Gudrid lived, according to *Eirik the Red's Saga*) in 1295, but there are references to six women who became anchoresses in Iceland before the establishment of proper convents. See also *Eirik the Red's Saga* note 35.

21. *Bishop Brand ... Bishop Bjorn*: Brand Saemundarson was bishop of Holar in the north of Iceland, 1163–1201. Bishop Thorlak Runolfsson was bishop of Skalholt in the south of Iceland, 1118–33; Ari the Learned consulted him when writing *The Book of the Icelanders* (see Introduction, p. xxix). Bishop Bjorn Gilsson was bishop of Holar, 1147–62.

EIRIK THE RED'S SAGA

1. *Halfdan White-leg ... Oppland*: Of the prominent Yngling royal family.

2. *declared himself king*: Irish sources mention Amlaíb as a king of the Viking settlement in Dublin, 853–71. Olaf (a cognate name) the White has often been identified with him. Olaf's wife, Aud, is not known outside Icelandic sources.

3. *daughter of Ketil Flat-nose*: Ketil Flat-nose had fled to the Hebrides in King Harald Fair-hair's time. One of his other daughters, Thorunn Hyrna, married a grandson of King Kjarval of Ireland, Helgi the Lean, and at least five of Ketil's children became leading settlers in Iceland, in the south, west and north. The royal connections established here at the beginning of the saga elevate the status of the descendant of both Aud the Deep-minded (the matriarch in *The Saga of the People of Laxardal*, Penguin Classics 2008) and King Kjarval: Thorfinn Karlsefni, the major male character (see Family Tree on pp. 72–73). They also emphasize the stark contrast in backgrounds of Karlsefni and his wife, Gudrid Thorbjarnardottir, the granddaughter of Vifil who was brought to Iceland by Aud as a bondsman.

4. *Earl Thorfinn the Skull-splitter*: I.e. Earl Thorfinn of Orkney (d. 963).

5. *in Britain*: The Icelandic expression meaning 'west of the sea' commonly refers to the lands west of the North Sea: the British Isles.

6. *Jorund Atlason*: Elsewhere said to be the son of Ulf and of Helgi the Lean's sister Bjorg, thus linking his daughter Thjodhild's and Eirik the Red's children with the Hebrides and Irish-Scandinavian royalty.

7. *Eiriksstadir by Vatnshorn*: Archaeologist Guðmundur Ólafsson has excavated a 50-square-metre hall at Eiriksstadir, which was lived in for a short while at the end of the tenth century, and was built in two stages; the hall was abandoned shortly after it was completed. It was fitted in at the eastern boundary of the family farm Vatnshorn, between two existing farms, and archaeological evidence about the history and location of the hall corroborates what the sagas say about Eirik the Red. (A conjectural replica has been constructed and is open to the public.)

8. *warlock songs*: The Icelandic *varðlok(k)ur* has been best

explained as derived from 'warlock', applied in the Scottish
islands to witches and magical incantations.

9. *and two sons, Thorstein and Leif*: The *Hauksbók* manuscript
    specifies that Eirik had two sons 'by her', i.e. Thjodhild – which
    must also be assumed here as Thorvald and Freydis, his daughter,
    appear later (Chapters 8, 11 and 12). All four children are intro-
    duced in *The Saga of the Greenlanders* (Chapter 1), but their
    mothers are not identified.

10. *hauntings at Froda*: See *The Saga of the People of Eyri* (Penguin
    Classics, 2003).

11. *self-sown wheat*: May refer to wild rice (*Zizania aquatica*) or
    wild rye (*Elymus virginicus*); the latter grows in the same area as
    the wild grapes (*Vitis riparia*), that is, in the southern regions of
    the Gulf of St Lawrence, and looks much like wheat. A similar
    remark is also found in Jacques Cartier's account from 1534
    when he explored Prince Edward Island in the Gulf of
    St Lawrence and came upon 'wild oats like rye, which one would
    say had been sown there and tilled' (H. P. Biggar (ed.), *The
    Voyages of Jacques Cartier* (Ottawa, 1924), p. 43). See Introduc-
    tion, p. xxxv.

12. *there were trees known as burl*: The writer in Iceland was prob-
    ably not familiar with burls on trees, so he uses the Nordic word
    for burl, *mösur*, as if it referred to a tree species. See *The Saga
    of the Greenlanders*, Chapter 8 and note 19. The *Hauksbók*
    manuscript adds that 'some of the trees were so large that they
    were used for building houses'.

13. *He converted the country to Christianity*: The *Hauksbók* manu-
    script expands: 'In so doing he showed his strong character and
    kindness, as in so many other things when he brought Christianity
    to the country [Greenland], and was afterwards called Leif the
    Lucky.'

14. *Thjodhild's church*: Archaeological excavations on the site of
    Brattahlid have revealed a church from the first decades of the
    settlement, surrounded by a Christian cemetery where nearly one
    hundred people were buried. (The church and the farm have now
    been reconstructed and are open to the public.)

15. *Karlsefni was a man of good family and good means*: The
    Hauksbók manuscript has a much more detailed account of
    Karlsefni's family, linking him with the characters in the intro-
    duction, that is, King Oleif the White in Dublin and Aud the
    Deep-minded – as well as King Kjarval of Ireland. Here the
    writer probably assumes that Thord Horse-head and his lineage

(established in other sources and packed with 'celebrities') are sufficiently well known for the audience to make the connection.

16. *Snorri Thorbrandsson*: Snorri's Vinland voyage is referred to in Chapter 48 of *The Saga of the People of Eyri*.

17. *Thorhall Gamlason*: Nicknamed 'Vinlander' in Chapters 14 and 30 of *The Saga of Grettir the Strong* (Penguin Classics, 2005).

18. *Vinland*: This is the first time that the saga mentions Vinland by name, clearly indicating that it assumed the audience knew the oral stories underlying the written saga. Listeners were expected to know that this story is about Vinland, and in particular about the voyage of Karlsefni and Gudrid, and to be aware that others had been there before them, including both Leif and his brother Thorvald.

19. *wide knowledge of the uninhabited regions*: The Nordic Greenlanders regularly ventured far north along the western coast of Greenland on hunting expeditions, both around Disco Island and beyond. They sold walrus tusks, laces and ropes of walrus skin, furs, gyrfalcons and narwhale teeth, and kept trade routes open between Iceland and mainland Scandinavia. However, towards the end of the settlement in Greenland, in the fifteenth century, the inhabitants probably traded directly with other Europeans. *The Greenland Chronicle*, written in Iceland in the seventeenth century, also recalls the hardships in the uninhabited regions of that country:

> The ice in Greenland on the western side is like high towers or cliffs and very uneven. No seals come with it. It is in the ice of this northerly sea that most ships were wrecked in earlier times, as shown by many accounts in *The Tale of Tosti*. Corpse-Lodin earned his name from ransacking the northern wild regions during the summers, bringing back south for church burial dead bodies of shipwrecked and icewrecked mariners whom he found in caves and craters. By their side were always carved runes that would tell of all their misfortune and torment.
>
> (Ólafur Halldórsson, *Grænland í miðaldaritum* (Reykjavík, 1978), p. 56)

Nordic artefacts from the medieval period have been discovered in the high arctic regions of north-east Canada. These hunting trips are distinct from the Vinland voyages.

20. *Bear islands*: Most often identified with Disco Island and other islands in that area.

21. *Helluland (Stone-slab land)*: Probably either Baffin Island or the northern regions of Labrador.

22. *Bjarney (Bear Island), and the forested land itself Markland*: The island now called Belle Isle is a well-known landmark for seafarers, south-east from the coast of the forested Labrador. It is reasonable to assume that the story is now passing Labrador and pointing out the main landmark off the shore, Bjarney.

23. *discovering the keel of a ship there*: The audience would know the story of Thorvald breaking the keel of his ship as related in *The Saga of the Greenlanders*, so this voyage has now extended far south of Leif's Camp in that saga. In view of what is said about Vinland in Chapter 9, it is clear that Kjalarnes (Keel Point) is east of Leif's Vinland and north of Straumsfjord (Stream fjord). Leif's Vinland is two days' sailing south-west over open sea from Markland (according to *The Saga of the Greenlanders*; see Introduction, pp. xxxii–xxxiv).

24. *a garment known as a kjafal*: This word (also written *bjafal*) may be cognate with the Gaelic *cabhail*, trunk of a shirt, or *giobal*, garment, or even derived from Old/Middle Irish *cochall*, cowl, hood, hooded cloak.

25. *Old Redbeard*: A common name for the god Thor.

26. *to seek Vinland*: Karlsefni has gone south beyond Leif's Vinland, which is reached by going north around Kjalarnes and heading west, as Karlsefni later does.

27. *flounder*: Icelandic *helgir fiskar* can refer to any type of flatfish. See Introduction, pp. xxxv–xxxvi.

28. *a large round object*: This has been compared with a throwing weapon known from Algonquin tribes in North America, described in the nineteenth century as a large boulder wrapped in skin and mounted on a pole (Birgitta Wallace, 'An Archaeologist's Interpretation of the Vinland Sagas', in *Vikings: The North Atlantic Saga*, ed. William W. Fitzhugh and Elisabeth I. Ward (Washington, DC, and London, 2000), p. 230).

29. *deer marrow blended with blood*: Explained as a description of pemmican, originally a native North American food consisting of dried meat, berries and fat.

30. *a one-legged creature*: It was commonly believed that there were unipeds in Africa, and some Icelanders speculated that Vinland was probably an extension of Africa, in which case the exit to the outer ocean that encircled the inhabited parts of earth would be between Markland and Vinland. Cartier also heard stories in

Canada about a land of unipeds – the age and origins of which are unknown.

31. *Vethild ... Ovaegi ... Avaldamon ... Valdidida*: These names have not been identified in native North American languages. However, they sound exotic in an Icelandic context and serve to create local verbal colour.

32. *the land of the white men*: *The Book of Settlements* says that the 'Land of the White Men' is six days' sailing west from Ireland, and the *Hauksbók* manuscript has the name 'Ireland the Great' here. This links up with Irish tales about a wondrous land in the west: *Tír na bhFear bhFionn* appears in post-medieval Irish sources and means literally 'Land of the White Men'. See Introduction, p. xii.

33. *after which they told this tale*: As the audience can deduce from *The Saga of the Greenlanders* about the danger involved (Chapter 4), the message of this story is clear. See Introduction, p. xxx.

34. *Bishop Thorlak Runolfsson ... Bishop Brand*: See *The Saga of the Greenlanders* note 21.

35. *And here ends this saga*: The *Hauksbók* manuscript adds a genealogy, written by lawspeaker Hauk Erlendsson in the early 1300s, in which he traces nine generations from Gudrid and Karlsefni to himself and also to Hallbera, who founded the convent at Reynines in Skagafjord and was abbess there 1299–1330 (see *The Saga of the Greenlanders* note 20).

MAPS

1. Bjarni Herjolfsson's voyage in *The Saga of the Greenlanders*

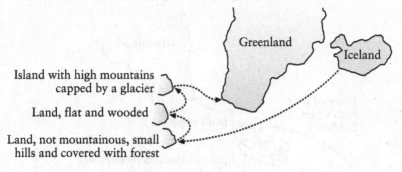

Island with high mountains capped by a glacier

Land, flat and wooded

Land, not mountainous, small hills and covered with forest

2. Leif Eiriksson's voyage in *The Saga of the Greenlanders*

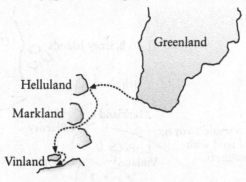

Island north of the land, with sweet dews, headland stretching northwards from the land, sound between the island and the headland, extensive shallows, salmon river, sea-lagoon, grapes and timber

Mental maps of the New World in *The Vinland Sagas*

3. Thorvald Eiriksson's voyage in *The Saga of the Greenlanders*

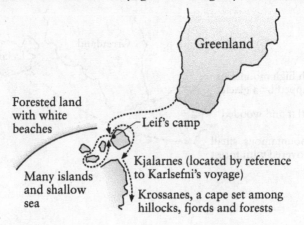

Greenland

Forested land with white beaches

Leif's camp

Kjalarnes (located by reference to Karlsefni's voyage)

Many islands and shallow sea

Krossanes, a cape set among hillocks, fjords and forests

4. Karlsefni's and Gudrid's voyage in *Eirik the Red's Saga*

Bjarney Islands

Greenland

Helluland

Markland

(from Thorvald's voyage: Forested land with white beaches)

Bjarney

Leif's Vinland

Kjalarnes (Keel Point)

Land of the One-Legged

Stream Fjord/Stream Island

River flowing from the east

Mountains

Headland with animals

Hop/Tidal pool

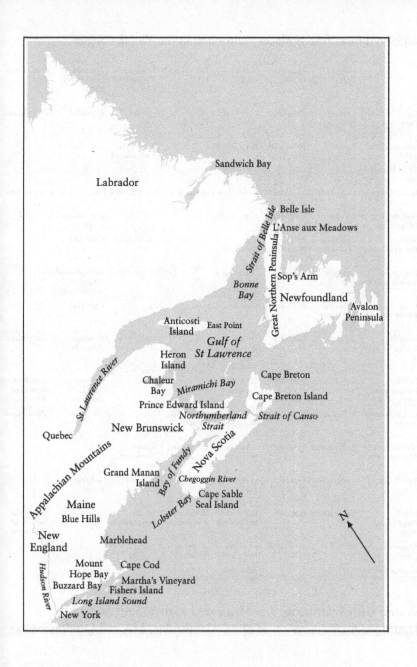

Suggested locations of places mentioned in the *Vinland Sagas*

	Helluland GS/ES	Markland GS/ES	Vinland GS/ES	Leif's camp GS	Krossanes (Crosspoint) GS	Kjalarnes (Keel Point) GS/ES	Bear Islands ES
Carl Christian Rafn 1837	Labrador/Newfoundland	Nova Scotia	Cape Cod region	Mount Hope Bay	on Cape Cod	Cape Cod	Disco Island
Gustav Storm 1887	Labrador	Newfoundland	Nova Scotia		north Cape Breton Island	Cape Breton	
M. L. Fernald 1910			Labrador				
Fridtjof Nansen 1911	Considered *The Vinland Sagas* to be based on European legends of blessed islands in the western ocean.						
William H. Babcock 1913	Labrador	Newfoundland	Nova Scotia			Cape Breton Island	
William Hovgaard 1914	Baffin Island / Labrador	Labrador / Nova Scotia	near Cape Cod	on Cape Cod	Marblehead	Cape Cod	
Hans P. Steensby 1918	Labrador	Labrador	St Lawrence valley		near to Hop	on north coast of Gulf of St Lawrence	
G. M. Gathorne-Hardy 1921	Labrador/Newfoundland	Nova Scotia	Cape Cod			Cape Cod	
Matthías Þórðarson 1930, 1935	Labrador	Labrador	New England / New Brunswick		mouth of St. Lawrence	on Gaspé Peninsula	Disco Island
Halldór Hermannsson 1927, 1936	Labrador	Labrador	New England			Anticosti Island, East Point	near Western Settlement (Greenland)
Helge Ingstad 1985	Baffin Island	Labrador	L'Anse aux Meadows	L'Anse aux Meadows			Disco Island
Samuel Eliot Morison 1971	Baffin Island	Labrador	L'Anse aux Meadows	L'Anse aux Meadows	western Newfoundland		
Erik Wahlgren 1986	Baffin Island	Labrador/Newfoundland	in Bay of Fundy	in Bay of Fundy	in Bay of Fundy	in Bay of Fundy	
Páll Bergþórsson 2000	Baffin Island	Labrador	mouth of St Lawrence	L'Anse aux Meadows	on Cape Breton Island		near Western Settlement (Greenland)
Mats G. Larsson 1999	Labrador	Newfoundland	southern Nova Scotia	L'Anse aux Meadows			
Birgitta Wallace 2000			Miramichi Bay	L'Anse aux Meadows			

Source: Gísli Sigurðsson, *The Medieval Icelandic Saga and Oral Tradition: A Discourse on Method* (Cambridge, MA and London, 2004)

Bjarney II ES	Furdustrandir (Wonder Beaches) ES	Straumsfjord (Stream Fjord) ES	Straumsey (Stream Island) ES	Hop ES	Land of the One-Legged ES	Mountains (seen from Hop and Land of the One-Legged) ES
Cape Sable	Cape Cod	Buzzard Bay	Martha's Vineyard	Mount Hope Bay		Blue Hills
	Cape Breton Island	Strait of Canso		southern Nova Scotia		
Avalon Peninsula	Nova Scotia	Bay of Fundy	Grand Manan Island	Mount Hope Bay	west Cape Breton Island	
	southern Labrador peninsula	Sandwich Bay		Sop's Arm	Bonne Bay	Great Northern Peninsula
Great Northern Peninsula	southern Labrador peninsula	mouth of St Lawrence				Gaspé Peninsula
Nova Scotia	Cape Cod	Long Island Sound	Fishers Island	mouth of Hudson River		
Belle Isle	southern Labrador peninsula	Northumberland Strait		New England	north of St Lawrence River	Appalachians
Belle Isle	southern Labrador peninsula	Chaleur Bay	Heron Island	New England	mouth of St Lawrence	Gaspé Peninsula
	southern Labrador peninsula	Strait of Belle Isle		L'Anse aux Meadows		
	southern Labrador peninsula	Strait of Belle Isle	Belle Isle	eastern Newfoundland	western Newfoundland	Great Northern Peninsula
	southern Labrador peninsula	Strait of Belle Isle	Belle Isle	south of Newfoundland		
Anticosti Island	Nova Scotia	Bay of Fundy	Grand Manan Island	mouth of Hudson River	mouth of St Lawrence	Appalachians
	Nova Scotia	Lobster Bay	Seal Island	Chegoggin River	western Cape Breton Island	Nova Scotia
		Strait of Belle Isle	Belle Isle	Miramichi Bay		

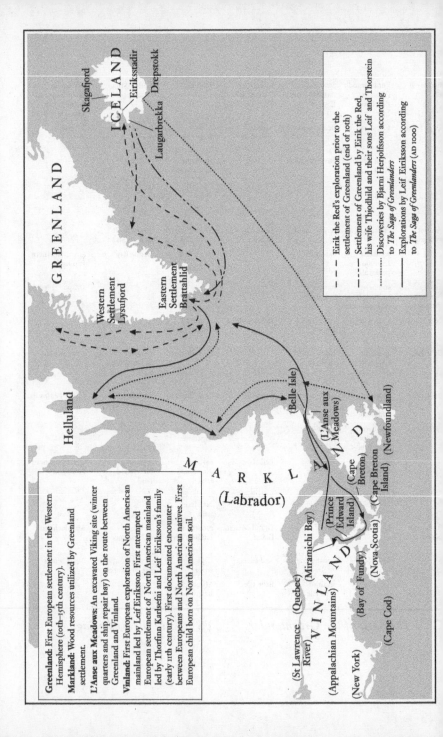

Greenland: First European settlement in the Western Hemisphere (10th–15th century).

Markland: Wood resources utilized by Greenland settlement.

L'Anse aux Meadows: An excavated Viking site (winter quarters and ship repair bay) on the route between Greenland and Vinland.

Vinland: First European exploration of North American mainland led by Leif Eiriksson. First attempted European settlement of North American mainland led by Thorfinn Karlsefni and Leif Eiriksson's family (early 11th century). First documented encounter between Europeans and North American natives. First European child born on North American soil.

- – – – Eirik the Red's exploration prior to the settlement of Greenland (end of 10th)
- – · – · Settlement of Greenland by Eirik the Red, his wife Thjodhild and their sons Leif and Thorstein
- · · · · · · Discoveries by Bjarni Herjolfsson according to *The Saga of Greenlanders*
- ——— Explorations by Leif Eiriksson according to *The Saga of Greenlanders* (AD 1000)

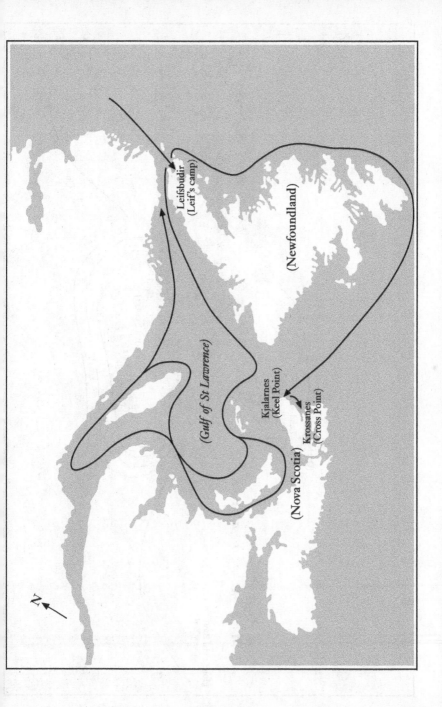

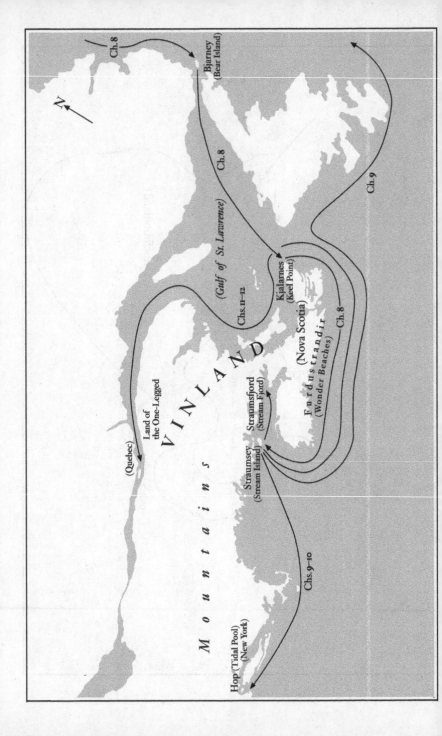

N

Ch. 8

Bjarney
(Bear Island)

Ch. 8

Ch. 9

(Gulf of St. Lawrence)

Chs. 11–12

Kjalarnes
(Keel Point)

Furdustrandir
(Wonder Beaches)

Ch. 8

Land of
the One-Legged

V I N L A N D

(Quebec)

Straumsfjord
(Stream Fjord)

(Nova Scotia)

M o u n t a i n s

Straumsey
(Stream Island)

Chs. 9–10

Hop (Tidal Pool)
(New York)

FAMILY TREE

Origins and family relations of the main Vinland explorers

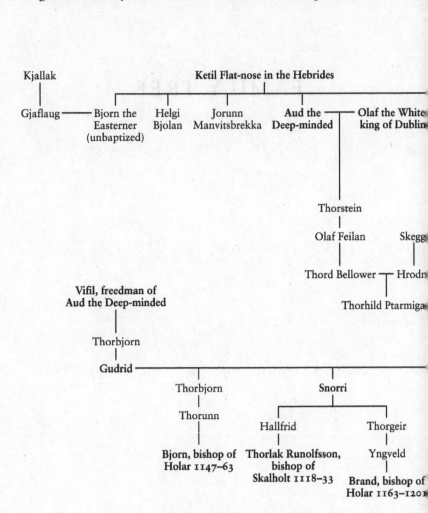

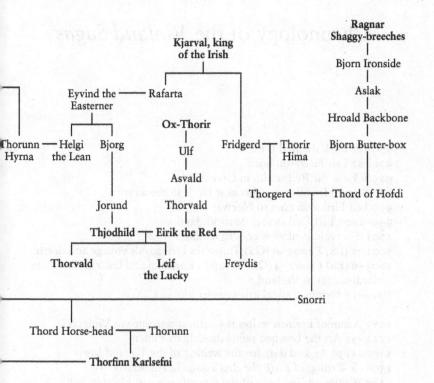

Chronology of the *Vinland Sagas*

940–50 Eirik the Red born
970–80 Leif Eiriksson born
985/6 Eirik the Red settles in Greenland
999 Bjarni Herjolfsson sights new lands in the west
999 Leif Eiriksson goes to Norway
999–1000 Leif Eiriksson goes to Vinland
1001 Thorvald Eiriksson goes to Vinland
1001–2 (ES) / 1005–6 (GS) Thorstein Eiriksson's voyage and death
1003–6 (ES) / 1007–9 (GS) Thorfinn Karlsefni and Gudrid Thorbjarnardottir go to Vinland
1010–11 Freydis Eiriksdottir goes to Vinland

1075 Adam of Bremen writes the earliest reference to Vinland
1122–32 Ari the Learned refers directly to Vinland
1200–1250 Argued date for the writing of the *Vinland Sagas*
1306–8 Writing of *Eirik the Red's Saga* in *Hauksbók*
1387 Writing of *The Saga of the Greenlanders* in *Flateyjarbók*
1420–50 Writing of *Eirik the Red's Saga* in *Skálholtsbók*

ES = *Eirik the Red's Saga*
GS = *The Saga of the Greenlanders*

Ships

No full-sized ships have been found in excavations in Iceland, only small boats which have been placed in graves. Several types of ships are mentioned in the sagas, however, and it is obvious that they had a variety of purposes, ranging from the local ferrying of travellers to foreign warfare, trade and the transportation of cargo across the open sea.

It is worth noting that, unlike today's ocean-going vessels, the ships of this time were open to the elements and had no decks in the modern sense of the word. Navigation was largely carried out by means of the sun, stars, landmarks, and knowledge of birds and whales. The ships were propelled by the wind (with the use of large sails) and human strength (through the use of oars). They were steered by a single rudder which was attached to the starboard side of the vessel, near the stern.

There seems to have been a distinction, though not a firm one, between a 'ship' and a 'boat', in that a ship (*skip*) was seen as being a vessel that usually had more than twelve oars, while a boat (*bátur*) had fewer than twelve. There was no sharp difference between warships and trading ships, since trading ships were sometimes used for warfare. Nonetheless, warships tended to be large, long and slender, and designed for both sailing and rowing. They were usually divided laterally into spaces for pairs of rowers, known as *rúm* (literally 'rooms'). The warships of kings, such as the famous Long Serpent and Bison belonging to Olaf Tryggvason and Olaf Haraldsson of Norway, often had more than thirty 'rooms', that is more than sixty oars. Trading vessels tended to be somewhat different.

All trading ships were broader in proportion to their length than warships. They had a rounder form, a bigger freeboard and a deeper draught than the longships. As they were designed almost exclusively for sailing, in most cases the mast was fixed. On the permanent deck fore and aft it was

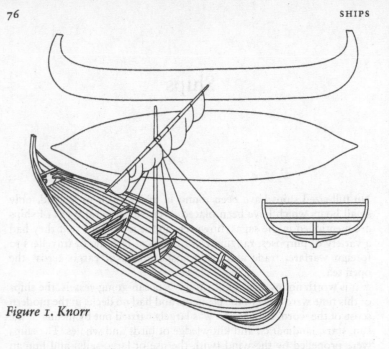

Figure 1. Knorr

possible to stand or sit in a row if necessary, for here (but not amidships)
there were oar-holes in the ship's side. All the middle part of the ships
was occupied by the cargo.

(Brøgger and Shetelig, p. 179)

It is unlikely that warships ever sailed to Iceland, but the saga heroes
are often said to have gone raiding on their trips abroad. The most
important ship for the Icelanders was the knorr (*knörr*). Smaller, broad
boats of a similar kind were used for centuries in Iceland, especially
in the area around Breidafjord. Such boats might well be similar to
the smaller cargo vessels (*byrðingar*) mentioned in the sagas.

The most common ships

The cargo vessel was short and broad, smaller than the knorr, and
mainly intended for coastal trade, although on occasion such vessels
seem to have been ocean-going. They tended to have crews of between
twelve and twenty men. The vessel known as Skuldelev 3, like the
other Skuldelev ships now on display in Roskilde, is probably an
example of a cargo vessel. It is *c.* 13.8m long and 3.3m in the beam.

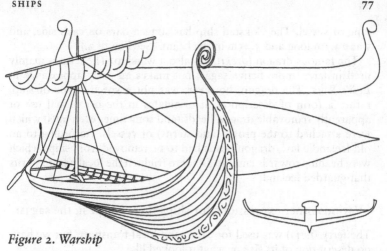

Figure 2. Warship

The knorr was a large, wide-bodied, sturdy, ocean-going cargo ship, the biggest of the trading ships. The settlers of Iceland and Greenland, and the Vinland explorers, seem to have most commonly used the knorr, which was capable of carrying not only people but also live-stock, cargo and large amounts of supplies. An example of the knorr (referred to as Skuldelev 1) was found in Roskilde fjord in Denmark and is on display in Roskilde. This is *c.* 16.3m long and *c.* 4.5m in the beam. (See Figure 1.)

The expression longship (*langskip*) was a collective, general term used for large warships, more than thirty-two oars. Some of these were of great size, like King Olaf Tryggvason's Long Serpent, which is said to have had thirty-four 'rooms', making a total of sixty-eight oarsmen, and probably also had space for additional warriors. As in the case of the warship (*karfi*) (see below), the size was usually indicated by the number of places for rowers. The ship known as Skuldelev 2, now on display in Roskilde, is thought to be a longship. This vessel, which probably was 28–9m long and *c.* 4.5m in the beam, might have carried between fifty and sixty men. Nonetheless, it is somewhat smaller than many of the Norwegian longships described in the sagas.

The warship was generally smaller than the longships owned by kings and great chieftains. The size clearly varied: they range from a warship with sixteen oars on each side, mentioned in the *Saga of Grettir the Strong*, to the warship with six oars on each side which is said to have been owned by a child in *Egil's Saga*. The Gokstad and Oseberg ships, on display in Oslo, have been identified as being this type of vessel. The Gokstad ship has sixteen oars on each side, and was 23.3m long and 5.25m in the beam. (See Figure 2.)

The famous dragon (*dreki*) was also a warship. The term is mainly used in later, more fictive sagas, but makes an early appearance in *Egil's Saga*. The dragon, however, was not a specific type of ship, rather a form of description. It originates in the occasional use of apparently removable dragon heads (and sometimes even tails) which were attached to the prows (and sterns) of vessels. According to an old Icelandic law, dragon heads had to be removed from ships which were heading towards land, so as not to frighten the local nature spirits that guarded Iceland.

Various other expressions for ships that appear in the sagas:

The ferry (*ferja*) was used for cargo and local transport, but we have no description of its size or what it looked like.

The general term trading vessel (*kaupskip*) simply refers to any vessel engaged in trade (*kaup*). The term was probably usually synonymous with the word knorr.

The expressions large warship (*skeið*), light ship/boat/smack (*skúta*) and swift warship (*snekkja*) are, as Brøgger and Shetelig have pointed out (p. 169), hardly classifications by size or equipment, but rather tend to be 'used merely in a transferred sense as indistinct imagery'.

See further:

Brøgger, A. W. and Shetelig, H., *The Viking Ships* (Oslo, 1951).
Foote, Peter and Wilson, D. M., *The Viking Achievement* (London, 1970).
Campbell, James Graham, *The Viking World* (London, 1980).

The Farm

The farm (*bær*) was a basic social and economic unit in Iceland. Although farms varied in size, there was presumably only one building on a 'farm' at the time of settlement, an all-purpose building known as a hall or farmhouse (*skáli*) or longhouse (*langhús*), constructed on the model of the farmhouses the settlers had inhabited in Norway. Over time, additional rooms and/or wings were often added to the original construction.

The Icelandic farmhouse shown in the illustrations is based on information provided by the excavations at Stong (Stöng) in the Thjorsardal valley in the south of Iceland. Stong is regarded as having been an average-sized farm by Icelandic standards. The settlement was abandoned as a result of the devastating ash-fall from the great eruption of Hekla in 1104.

The illustrations are intended to help readers visualize the farm, and understand the specialized vocabulary used to describe it. Some terms can be found in the Glossary.

The plan of the farmstead (Figure 3) shows an overall layout of a typical farm. It is based on measurements carried out by the archaeologist Daniel Bruun, but it should be stressed that the layout of these farms was far from fixed. Nonetheless, the plan indicates the common positioning of the haystack wall/yard (*stakkgarður*) in the often-mentioned hayfield (*tún*). The hayfield wall (*túngarður*) surrounds the farm and its hayfield.

Also placed outside the main farm are the animal sheds. With the exception of a cow shed, no barns or other animal sheds came to light at Stong, but these must have existed as they did on most farms. Sometimes they were attached to the farmhouse, but more often were independent constructions some distance away from the building. Sheep sheds, in particular, tended to be built farther away from the hall, and closer to the meadows used for grazing.

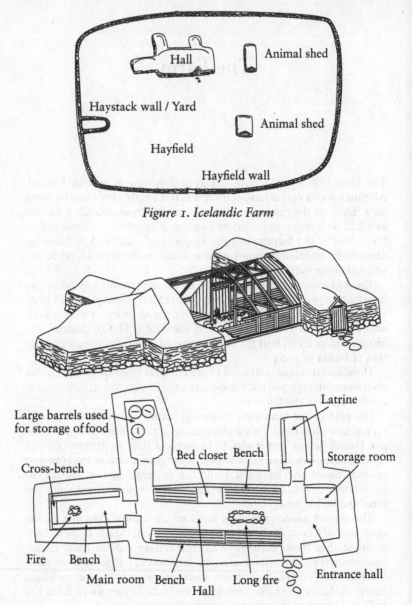

Figure 1. Icelandic Farm

Hall

Animal shed

Haystack wall / Yard

Animal shed

Hayfield

Hayfield wall

Large barrels used
for storage of food

Latrine

Cross-bench

Bed closet   Bench

Storage room

Fire   Bench

Main room   Bench

Hall

Long fire

Entrance hall

Figures 4 and 5. The Farmhouse at Stong

The smithy is also separate (for safety reasons), and the same often appears to have applied to the fire room/fire hall (*eldhús/eldaskáli*). The latter was essentially a form of specialized kitchen. It was not only used for cooking, but was also the site of other daily household activities carried out around the fire. Indeed, sometimes the term *eldhús* seems to refer not to a separate building, but to the farmhouse, instead of the word hall, stressing the presence of the fire and warmth in the living quarters.

Figure 4 is a cross-section of the hall at Stong, giving an idea of the way the buildings were constructed. The framework was timber. The main weight of the roof rested on beams, which, in turn, were supported by pillars on either side of the hall. The high-seat pillars (*öndvegissúlur*) that some settlers brought with them from Norway might have been related to the pillars placed on either side of the high seat (*hásæti*). The outer walls of most farms in Iceland were constructed of a thick layer of turf and stone, which served to insulate the building. The smoke from the main fire was usually let out through a vent in the roof, but the living quarters would still have been rather smoke-ridden.

Figure 5 depicts the layout of the farmhouse excavated at Stong. The purpose of the area here marked 'latrine' is uncertain, but this role makes sense on the basis of the layout of the room, and the description given in *The Tale of Thorstein Shiver*, for example.

See further:
Foote and Wilson, *The Viking Achievement*.
Campbell, *The Viking World*.

Social, Political and Legal Structure

The notion of kinship is central to the sense of honour and duty in the sagas, and thereby to their action. Kinship essentially involves a sense of belonging not unlike that underlying the Celtic clan systems. The Icelandic word for kin or clan (*ætt*) is cognate with other words meaning 'to own' and 'direction' – the notion could be described as a 'social compass'.

Establishing kinship is one of the justifications for the long genealogies, which tend to strike non-Icelandic readers as idiosyncratic detours, and also for the preludes in Norway before the main saga action begins. Members of the modern nuclear family or close relatives are only part of the picture, since kinsmen are all those who are linked through a common ancestor – preferably one of high birth and high repute – as far back as five or six generations or even more.

Marriage ties, sworn brotherhood and other bonds could create conflicting loyalties with respect to the duty of revenge. A strict order stipulated who was to take revenge within the fairly immediate family, with a 'multiplier effect' if those seeking vengeance were killed in the process. The obligation to take revenge was inherited, just like wealth, property and claims.

Patriarchy was the order of the day, although notable exceptions are found. Likewise, the physical duty of revenge devolved only upon males, but women were often responsible for instigating it, either by urging a husband or brother to action with slurs about their cowardice, or by bringing up their sons with a vengeful sense of purpose and even supplying them with old weapons that had become family heirlooms.

Iceland was unique among European societies in the tenth to thirteenth centuries in two respects in particular: it had no king, and no executive power to follow through the pronouncements of its highly sophisticated legislative and judicial institutions. The lack of executive power meant that there was no means for preventing men from taking the law into their own hands, which gave rise to many memorable conflicts recorded in the sagas, but also led to the gradual disintegration of the Commonwealth in the thirteenth century.

The Althing served not only as a general or national assembly (which is what its name means), but also as the main festival and social gathering of the year, where people exchanged stories and news, renewed acquaintances with old friends and relatives, and the like.

The accused generally did not attend the Thing, but was defended by someone else, who called witnesses and was entitled to disqualify members of the panel. Panels did not testify to the details and facts of the case in the modern sense, but determined whether the incident had taken place. The case was then summed up and a ruling passed on it by the Quarter Court.

Penalties depended upon the seriousness of the case and took the form of either monetary compensation or outlawry. A confiscation court would seize the belongings of a person outlawed for three years or life. Two types of outlawry were applied, depending upon the serious-ness of the offence: lesser outlawry (*fjörbaugsgarður*) and full outlawry (*skóggangur*). According to the legal code *Grágás*, a lesser outlaw enjoyed sanctuary in three homes in Iceland, no more than one day's passage from each other, and safe passage along a direct route between them, but was obliged to leave the country as soon as possible for three years' exile. A fine of one mark was also levied on the outlaw – *fjörbaugsgarður* means literally 'life-ring enclosure' and the penalty was originally a silver ring to be paid to the godi, the local chieftain, in charge of the court, as a token to save the offender's life, while the enclosure was his safe route into exile. A sentence of lesser outlawry was converted to full outlawry if he returned to Iceland before three years, if no passage was requested on his behalf or if he could not arrange to leave the country within three summers after sentence was passed on him.

Glossary

The Icelandic term is printed in italics after the head-word, with modern spelling.

ball-game *knattleikur*: A game played with a hard ball and a bat, possibly similar to the Gaelic game known as hurling, which is still played in Scotland and Ireland. The exact rules, however, are uncertain. See, for example, the description of the game in *Gisli Sursson's Saga*, chs. 15 and 18.

black Often used here to translate *blár*, which in modern Icelandic means only 'blue'.

board game *tafl*: *Tafl* probably often refers to chess, which had plainly reached Scandinavia before the twelfth century. However, in certain cases it might also refer to another board game known as *hnefatafl*. The rules of the latter game are uncertain, even though we know what the boards looked like.

booth *búð*: A temporary dwelling, often used by those who attended the various assemblies and ports of commerce. Structurally, it seems to have involved permanent walls which were covered by a tent-like roof, probably made of cloth.

directions *austur/vestur/norður/suður* (east/west/north/south): These directional terms are used in a very wide sense in the sagas; they are largely dependent on context, and they cannot always be trusted to reflect compass directions. Internationally, 'the east' generally refers to the countries to the east and south-east of Iceland, and although 'eastern' usually refers to a Norwegian, it can also apply to a Swede (especially since the concept of nationality was still not entirely clear when the sagas were being written), and might even be used for a person who has picked up Russian habits. 'The west', or to 'go west', tends to refer to Ireland and what are now the British Isles, but might even refer to lands even farther afield; the point of orientation is west of Norway. When confined to Iceland, directional terms sometimes refer to the quarter (Iceland was administratively divided into four parts based on the four cardinal directions) to which a person is travelling, e.g. a man going to the Althing (annual assembly in south Iceland) from the east of the country might be said to be going 'south' rather than the geographically more accurate 'west', and a person going home to the West Fjords from the Althing is said to be going 'west' rather than 'north'.

drapa *drápa*: A heroic, laudatory poem, usually in the complicated metre preferred by the Icelandic poets. Such poems were in fashion between the tenth and thirteenth centuries. They were usually composed in honour of kings, earls and other prominent men; or they might be directed towards a loved one, composed in memory of the deceased or in relation to some religious matter. A drapa usually consisted of three parts: an introduction, a middle section including one or more refrains, and a conclusion. It was usually clearly distinguished from the flokk, which tended to be shorter, less laudatory and without refrains (see *The Saga of Gunnlaug Serpent-tongue*, ch. 9). For an example of a drapa, see *Egil's Saga*, ch. 61.

earl *jarl*: Title generally restricted to men of high rank in northern countries (though not in Iceland), who could be independent rulers or subordinate to a king. The title could be inherited, or it could be conferred by a king on a prominent supporter or leader of military forces. The earls of Lade who appear in a number of sagas and tales ruled large sections of northern Norway (and often many southerly areas as well) for several centuries. Another prominent, almost independent, earldom was that of Orkney and Shetland.

east *austur*. See directions.

follower *hirðmaður*: A member of the inner circle of followers that surrounded the Scandinavian kings, a sworn king's man.

foster- *fóstur-, fóstri, fóstra*: Children during the saga period were often brought up by foster-parents, who received either payment or support in return from the real parents. Being fostered was therefore somewhat different from being adopted: it was essentially a legal agreement and, more importantly, a form of alliance. Nonetheless, fostered children were seen as being part of the family circle emotionally, and in some cases legally. Relationships and loyalties between foster-kindred could become very strong. It should be noted that the expressions *fóstri/fóstra* were also used for people who had the function of looking after, bringing up and teaching the children on the farm.

freed slave *lausingi, leysingi*: A slave could be set or bought free, and thus acquired the general status of a free man, although this status was low, since if he/she died with no heir, his/her inheritance would return to the original owner. The children of freed slaves, however, were completely free.

full outlawry *skóggangur*. Outlawry for life. One of the terms applied to a man sentenced to full outlawry was *skógarmaður*, which literally means 'forest man', even though in Iceland there was scant possibility of his taking refuge in a forest. Full outlawry simply meant banishment from civilized society, whether the local land district, the province or the whole country. It also meant the confiscation of the outlaw's property to pay the prosecutor, cover debts and sometimes provide an allowance for the dependants he had left behind. A full outlaw was to be neither fed nor offered shelter. According to one legal codex from Norway, it was 'as if he were dead'. He had lost all goods, and all rights. Wherever he went he could be killed without any legal redress. His children became illegitimate and his body was to be buried in unconsecrated ground.

games *leikar*: *Leikur* (sing.) in Icelandic contained the same breadth of meaning as 'game' in English. The games meetings described in the sagas would probably have included a whole range of 'play' activities. Essentially, they involved men's sports, such as wrestling, ball games, 'skin-throwing games', 'scraper games' and horse-fights. Games of this kind took place whenever people came together, and seem to have formed a regular feature of assemblies and other gatherings (including the Althing) and religious festivals such as the Winter Nights. Sometimes prominent men invited people together specifically to take part in games.

hauntings/ghosts/spirits *draugar, afturgöngur, haugbúar*: Ghosts in medieval Scandinavia were seen as being corporeal, and thus capable of wrestling or fighting with opponents. This idea is naturally associated with the ancient pagan belief in Scandinavia and elsewhere that the dead should be buried with the possessions that they were going to need in the next life, such as ships, horses and weapons: in some way, the body was going to live again and need these items. There are many examples in the sagas of people encountering or seeing 'living ghosts' inside grave mounds. These spirits were called *haugbúar* (literally 'mound-dwellers'). Because of the fear of spirits walking again and disturbing the living, there were various measures that could be taken to ensure some degree of peace and quiet for the living: see, for example, *Egil's Saga*, ch. 59, and *Gisli Sursson's Saga*, chs. 14 and 17.

high seat *öndvegi*: The central section of one bench in the hall (at the inner end, or in the middle of the 'senior' side, to the right as one entered) was the rightful high seat of the owner of the farm. Even though it is usually referred to in English as the 'high seat', this position was not necessarily higher in elevation, only in honour. Opposite the owner sat the guest of honour.

hundred *hundrað*: A 'long hundred' or one hundred and twenty. The expression, however, rarely refers to an accurate number, rather a generalized 'round' figure.

knorr *knörr*: An ocean-going cargo vessel: see also 'Ships'.

lawspeaker *lögsögumaður, lögmaður*: *lögsögumaður* means literally 'the man who recites the law', referring to the time before the advent of writing when the lawspeaker had to learn the law by heart and recite one-third of it every year, perhaps at the Law Rock. If he was unsure about the text, he had to consult a team of five or more 'lawmen' (*lögmenn*) who knew the law well. The lawspeaker presided over the assembly at the *Althing* (general assembly) and was responsible for the preservation and clarification of legal tradition. He could exert influence, as in the case of the question about whether the Icelanders should accept Christianity (see *Njal's Saga*, ch. 105), but should not be regarded as having ruled the country. The power remained in the hands of the *godis* (the local chieftains who had legal and administrative responsibilities).

lesser outlawry *fjörbaugsgarður*: Differed from full or greater outlawry in that the lesser outlaw was only banished from society for three years. Furthermore, his land was not confiscated, and money was put aside to support his family. This made it possible for him to return later and continue a normal life. *Fjörbaugsgarður* means literally 'life-ring enclosure'. 'Life-ring' refers to the silver ring that the outlaw originally had to pay the godi in order to spare his life. (This was later fixed at a value of one mark.) 'Enclosure' refers to three sacrosanct homes no more than one day's journey from each other where the outlaw was permitted to stay while he arranged passage out of Iceland. He was allowed limited movement along the tracks directly joining these farms, and en route to the ship which would take him abroad. Anywhere else the outlaw was fair game and could be killed without redress. He had to leave the country and begin his sentence within the space of three summers after the verdict, but once abroad retained normal rights.

magic rite *seiður*: The exact nature of magic ritual, or *seiður*, is somewhat obscure. It appears that it was originally only practised by women. Although there are several accounts of males who performed this rite (including the god Odin), they are almost always looked down on as having engaged in an 'effeminate' activity. The magic rite seems to have had two main purposes: a spell to influence people or the elements (as in *The Saga of the People of Laxardal*, chs. 35–7, and *Gisli Sursson's Saga*, ch. 18), and a means of finding out about the future (as in *Eirik the Red's Saga*, ch. 4). There are evidently parallels between *seiður* and shamanistic rituals such as those carried out by the Lapps and Native Americans. See also seeress.

main room *stofa*: A room off the hall of a farmhouse.

mark *mörk*: A measurement of weight, eight ounces, approximately 214 grams.

north *norður*. See directions.

outlawry *útlegð, skóggangur, fjörbaugsgarður*: Two of the Icelandic words, *útlegð*, literally meaning 'lying, or sleeping, outside', and *skóggangur*, 'forest-walking', stress the idea of the outlaw having been ejected from the safe boundaries of civilized society and being forced to live in the wild, alongside the animals and nature spirits, little better than an animal himself. The word *útlagi* ('outlaw') is closely related to *útlegð*, but has also taken on the additional meaning of 'outside the law', which for early Scandinavians was synonymous with 'lying outside society'. Law was what made society. See also full outlawry and lesser outlawry.

seeress *völva*: The magic rites (*seiður*) performed by male magicians were essentially, and originally, a female activity. For a detailed account of a seeress using such a rite to gain knowledge of the future, see *Eirik the Red's Saga*, ch. 4. Seeresses could also gain such knowledge by 'sitting outside' (*útiseta*) at night on graves, at crossroads or at other powerful natural sites. The most famous examples of prophecies in Old Icelandic literature are the eddic poems *Völuspá* (The Prophecy of the Seeress) and *Baldurs draumar* (The Dreams of Balder), both of which deal with the coming of Ragnarok ('the fate of the gods'). See also magic rite.

slave *þræll*: Slavery was quite an important aspect of Viking Age trade. A large number of slaves were taken from the Baltic nations and the western European countries that were raided and invaded by Scandinavians between the eighth and eleventh centuries. In addition, the Scandinavians had few scruples against taking slaves from the other Nordic countries. Judging from their names and appearance, a large number of the slaves mentioned in the sagas seem to have come from Ireland and Scotland. Stereotypically they are presented in the sagas as being stupid and lazy. The eddic poem *Rígsþula* (The Chant of Rig) describes the mythical origins and the characteristics of the four main Scandinavian classes: the slaves, the farmers, the aristocracy and the kings. By law, slaves had hardly any rights at all, and they and their families could only be freed if their owners chose to do so, or somebody else bought their freedom: see freed slave. In the Icelandic Commonwealth, a slave who was wounded was entitled to one-third of the compensation money; the rest went to his owner.

sleeping-sack *húðfat*: A large leather bag used by travellers for sleeping.

south *suður*: See directions.

west *vestur*: See directions.

Winter Nights *veturnatur*: The period of two days when the winter began, around the middle of October. This was a particularly holy time of the year, when sacrifices were made to the female guardian spirits known as *dísir*, and other social activities such as games, meetings and weddings often took place.

Indexes of Characters and Places

CHARACTERS

PLACES

PENGUIN CLASSICS

THE SAGA OF GRETTIR THE STRONG

'The most valiant man who has ever lived in Iceland'

Composed at the end of the fourteenth century by an unknown author, *The Saga of Grettir the Strong* is one of the last great Icelandic sagas. It relates the tale of Grettir, an eleventh-century warrior struggling to hold on to the values of a heroic age as they are eclipsed by Christianity and a more pastoral lifestyle. Unable to settle into a community of farmers, Grettir becomes the aggressive scourge of both honest men and evil monsters – until, following a battle with the sinister ghost Glam, he is cursed to endure a life of tortured loneliness away from civilization, fighting giants, trolls and berserks. A mesmerizing combination of pagan ideals and Christian faith, this is a profoundly moving conclusion to the Golden Age of saga writing.

This is an updated edition of Bernard Scudder's acclaimed translation. The new introduction by Örnólfur Thorsson considers the influence of Christianity on Icelandic saga writing, and this edition also includes genealogical tables and a note on the translation.

Translated by Bernard Scudder

Edited with an introduction by Örnólfur Thorsson

PENGUIN CLASSICS

EGIL'S SAGA

'The sea-goddess has ruffled me,
stripped me bare of my loved ones'

Egil's Saga tells the story of the long and brutal life of the tenth-century warrior-poet and farmer Egil Skallagrimsson: a psychologically ambiguous character who was at once the composer of intricately beautiful poetry and a physical grotesque capable of staggering brutality. This Icelandic saga recounts Egil's progression from youthful savagery to mature wisdom as he struggles to defend his honour in a running feud against the Norwegian King Erik Blood-axe, fights for the English King Athelstan in his battles against Scotland and embarks on colourful Viking raids across Europe. Exploring issues as diverse as the question of loyalty, the power of poetry and the relationship between two brothers who love the same woman, *Egil's Saga* is a fascinating depiction of a deeply human character, and one of the true masterpieces of medieval literature.

This new translation by Bernard Scudder fully conveys the poetic style of the original. It also contains a new introduction by Svanhildur Óskarsdóttir, placing the saga in historical context, a detailed chronology, a chart of Egil's ancestors and family, maps and notes.

Translated by Bernard Scudder

Edited by Ornulfur Thorsson

THE STORY OF PENGUIN CLASSICS

Before 1946 ... 'Classics' are mainly the domain of academics and students; readable editions for everyone else are almost unheard of. This all changes when a little-known classicist, E. V. Rieu, presents Penguin founder Allen Lane with the translation of Homer's *Odyssey* that he has been working on in his spare time.

1946 Penguin Classics debuts with *The Odyssey*, which promptly sells three million copies. Suddenly, classics are no longer for the privileged few.

1950s Rieu, now series editor, turns to professional writers for the best modern, readable translations, including Dorothy L. Sayers's *Inferno* and Robert Graves's unexpurgated *Twelve Caesars*.

1960s The Classics are given the distinctive black covers that have remained a constant throughout the life of the series. Rieu retires in 1964, hailing the Penguin Classics list as 'the greatest educative force of the twentieth century.'

1970s A new generation of translators swells the Penguin Classics ranks, introducing readers of English to classics of world literature from more than twenty languages. The list grows to encompass more history, philosophy, science, religion and politics.

1980s The Penguin American Library launches with titles such as *Uncle Tom's Cabin*, and joins forces with Penguin Classics to provide the most comprehensive library of world literature available from any paperback publisher.

1990s The launch of Penguin Audiobooks brings the classics to a listening audience for the first time, and in 1999 the worldwide launch of the Penguin Classics website extends their reach to the global online community.

The 21st Century Penguin Classics are completely redesigned for the first time in nearly twenty years. This world-famous series now consists of more than 1300 titles, making the widest range of the best books ever written available to millions – and constantly redefining what makes a 'classic'.

The Odyssey continues ...

The best books ever written

PENGUIN (🐧) CLASSICS

SINCE 1946

Find out more at www.penguinclassics.com